Revolution and
A series of facsimile re
Jonathan Wordswoi

CW00342076

Wollstonecraft
Original Stories from Real Life 1791

Mary Wollstonecraft

Original Stories from Real Life

1791

Woodstock Books
Otley · Washington D.C.
2001

First published in this series 1990.
This new edition with revised introduction
published 2001 by
Woodstock Books
Otley, West Yorkshire
England LS21 3JP
and
Books International
PO Box 605, Herndon
VA 20172, U.S.A.

ISBN 1 85477 261 9 (cloth)
        1 85477 262 7 (paper)

Reproduced by permission from a copy in
The Bodleian Library, Oxford, shelfmark Vet A5f 1065
Introduction copyright © 2001 Jonathan Wordsworth

British Library Cataloguing-in-Publication Data
A catalogue record for this book is
available from the British Library

Library of Congress Cataloging-in-Publication Data
applied for

Printed and bound in England by
Smith Settle
Otley LS21 3JP

Introduction

Joseph Johnson's 1791 reissue of *Original Stories*, with
new plates by Blake, coincided with the rise of
Wollstonecraft as a political writer. Her *Vindication of the
Rights of Men* had been first of the many replies to
Burke's *Reflections on the Revolution in France*, appearing
within a month in December 1790. Now she was at
work on the famous second *Vindication* – of the *Rights of
Woman* (published 1792). In such a context, the 1788
Original Stories, with its pervading moral emphasis,
might seem out of place. But in fact Wollstonecraft's
values had changed very little. The education for which
she argues so passionately in *The Rights of Woman* is
designed to create God-fearing wives and mothers, not
political activists. Her new partnership with Blake is of
considerable importance. After his long apprenticeship
to the engraver James Basire, Blake had become an
accomplished (if rather old-fashioned) craftsman,
producing for Johnson book-illustrations from the
designs of Stothard and others. Alongside this
commercial engraving he had etched and illuminated
The Songs of Innocence and *Thel* in 1789, and *The
Marriage of Heaven and Hell* in 1790.

Like the *Songs of Innocence, Original Stories* is intended
for the moral improvement of children. In the words of
the title page, the conversations it contains are
'calculated to regulate the affections, and form the mind
to truth and goodness'. Wollstonecraft had all the right
qualifications. Five years' experience of running a
school had been followed in 1786-7 by a time in the
uncomfortable role of governess to an aristocratic
family. Both *Thoughts on the Education of Daughters*
(1787) and her autobiographical novel, *Mary: a fiction*
(1788), show her preoccupation with training the mind

to cope rationally with suffering and injustice. As the location of her school she had chosen Newington Green, an outlying village north of London, and home of Richard Price. It is arguable that Price – aside from Priestley, the leading dissenter of his day – was the greatest intellectual influence on her life. She did not concern herself with his theology (faith was for her largely instinctual), but adopted from him the dissenter's proud and positive attitudes to exclusion. Denied the vote, barred from the Universities and public life, dissenters occupied a position in society close to that of the would-be independent woman. Far from being put down, however, they formed in the 1780s an intellectual elite.

'Few are the modes of earning a subsistence', Wollstonecraft comments in *Thoughts on the Education of Daughters*, 'and those very humiliating'. She is thinking of the experience of women in her own position, educated, unmarried and without money. To be the 'humble companion of some rich old cousin' is to be betwixt and between, 'above the servants, yet considered by them as a spy, and ever reminded of her inferiority when in conversation with the superiors'. Seen in this light, the single woman's two alternatives are no less degrading:

A teacher at a school is only a kind of upper servant, who has more work than the menial ones.

[Life as] a governess to young ladies is equally disagreeable … The children treat [one] with disrespect, and often with insolence. In the mean time life glides away, and the spirits with it … (*Thoughts on the Education of Daughters* 1787, pp. 71-72)

Wollstonecraft's answer to this, and to the frequently worse subservience of marriage, is that women must 'be taught to think'. 'Thinking', she adds, 'is a severe exercise' – and she means it. At this early stage of her career we are offered no political solutions, just obedience to the will of God. 'Adversity is mercifully sent us to force us to think':

A sensible, delicate woman, who by some strange accident or mistake, is joined to a fool or brute, must be wretched beyond all names of wretchedness, if her views are confined to the present scene. Of what importance, then, is intellectual improvement, when our comfort here, and happiness hereafter, depends upon it.

Original Stories belongs to a long-established tradition. The volume may surprise us two hundred years later with its moral earnestness, but by the standards of Day's *Sandford and Merton*, or Hannah More's *Cheap Repository Tracts*, its piety is not excessive. Godwin in his *Memoirs* of *the Author of A vindication of the Rights of Woman* chooses to play down Wollstone-craft's faith (reporting with pleasure that she never referred to religion on her deathbed). But, for her, reason is a God-given faculty that leads the individual to virtue, and finally to eternal life. *Original Stories* is written on the assumption that teaching is a form of rescue. The author's task is 'to cure those faults by reason, which ought never to have taken root in the infant mind'. Mrs Mason, who tells the stories, is a paragon. Mary and Caroline, who listen, are 'shamefully ignorant'. Having been brought up largely by servants, they possess 'every prejudice that the vulgar casually instill' (one might think Wollstonecraft not entirely without prejudice herself). Mary is fourteen, Caroline twelve. They have 'tolerable capacities', but Mary has 'a turn for ridicule and Caroline [is] vain of her person'. To the modern reader the girls seem venial in their faults, astonishingly willing to accept correction (after spending her pocket-money on 'paltry ornaments', Caroline suffers anguish at not being able to give it to the poor), and positively avid in their response to cautionary tales.

Mrs Mason is relentless. Crazy Robin dies in a cave – finally. Before that he has been thrown unjustly into gaol, and lost his wife and two children from putrid fever. The two remaining children join him in his cell, and die there (giving Blake scope for a harrowing plate). Now mad, Robin escapes with his dog, to live on berries in his cave until the dog is shot by 'a young gentleman' whose horse it has barked at. Then he dies too:

'Was that the cave?' said Mary. They ran to it. 'Poor Robin! Did you ever hear of any thing so cruel?' 'Yes', answered Mrs Mason, 'and as we walk home I will relate an instance of still greater barbarity.'   (p. 27)

There follows the case of the Bastille prisoner, whose only friend – a spider – is crushed by the gaoler on orders from above.

Alongside Mrs Mason's tales there are the conversations that she holds with her charges, and the 'histories' they hear as they walk an area densely populated with the God-fearing and the grateful-in-adversity. Sailor Jack, for instance, on his crutches:

My poor captain! a better never plowed the ocean, he fell overboard too, and it was some time before we missed him; for it was quite dark, except that flashes of lightning, now and then, gave us light. I was at the helm, lashing it to the side of the ship – a dreadful flash came across me, and I lost one of my precious eyes. But thank God I have one left.   (p.70)

Surviving near-death in a French prison, and the loss of his dog and his legs saving others in a shipwreck, Jack lives to bring Mrs Mason to tears of benevolence:

standing in the water so long, I lost the use of my limbs – yet Heaven was good to me; Madam, there, sent a cart for us all, and took care of us; but I never recovered the use of my limbs. So she asked me all about my misfortunes, and sent for wife, who came directly, and we have lived here ever since. We catch fish for Madam, and I watch for a storm, hoping some time or another to be as kind to a poor perishing soul as she has been to me. Indeed we are very happy – I might now have been begging about the streets but for Madam, God bless her.

A tear strayed down Mrs Mason's cheek, while a smile of benevolence lighted up her countenance – the little girls caught each hand – They were all silent a few minutes ...   (pp.73-4)

It is the words 'Indeed we are very happy' that Blake chooses to illustrate. The two girls (far too small for their ages) bury their faces in Mrs Mason's lap, as she sits demure, straight-backed but with her eyes cast down, in the Sailor's neat and tidy parlour.

Blake's half-dozen illustrations add greatly to the volume. Crazy Robin stands rigid and abstracted above the corpses of his children, laid out upon the strangely short prison-bed as if upon a monument. A dog, woolly and lamb-like, licks his hand unnoticed. The same powerful stylization is present in the frontispiece, where Mary and Caroline lose completely their individuality to fit beneath the outstretched sheltering arms of their Good Angel. *Be calm, my child* has perhaps the most satisfying Blakean composition, and admits a tenderness such as Mrs Mason (in the text) very rarely shows. It has always been held that Wollstonecraft's feminism was an influence on *Visions of the Daughters of Albion* (1793); it seems very possible that there may be an earlier verbal borrowing in *The Marriage of Heaven and Hell*. We read in the Preface to *Original Stories* of 'the senses, the first inlets to the heart' ('inlet', 1788). Denouncing 'All Bibles or sacred codes' as the causes of error, the voice of the Devil proclaims in Plate 4 of the *Marriage*

Man has no body distinct from his Soul for that call'd body is a portion of Soul discerned by the five senses, *the chief inlets of Soul* in this age.

Others had used 'inlet' in not dissimilar ways, but to have it applied in each case to the senses makes the coincidence more striking.

It is difficult to know whether the author of *Original Stories* would have been flattered by such a borrowing. If she saw her illustrator's original writing she must have thought him a little heterodox. Which is nothing to what Mrs Mason would have felt had she seen in the *Marriage* that 'Prisons are built with stones of Law, Brothels with bricks of Religion'.

J. W.

Blake

Look what a fine morning it is. — Insects,
Birds, & Animals, are all enjoying existence.

Published by J. Johnson, Sept.ʳ 1.ˢᵗ 1791.

ORIGINAL STORIES

FROM

REAL LIFE;

WITH

CONVERSATIONS,

CALCULATED TO

REGULATE THE AFFECTIONS,

AND

FORM THE MIND

TO

TRUTH AND GOODNESS.

BY MARY WOLLSTONECRAFT.

LONDON:

PRINTED FOR J. JOHNSON, NO. 72, ST.
PAUL'S CHURCH-YARD.

1791.

PREFACE.

THESE conversations and tales are accommodated to the present state of society; which obliges the author to attempt to cure those faults by reason, which ought never to have taken root in the infant mind. Good habits, imperceptibly fixed, are far preferable to the precepts of reason; but, as this task requires more judgment than generally falls to the lot of parents, substitutes must be sought for, and medicines given, when regimen would have answered the purpose much better. I believe those who examine their own minds, will readily agree with me, that reason, with difficulty, conquers settled habits, even when it is arrived at some degree of maturity: why then do we suffer children to be bound with fetters, which their half-formed faculties cannot break.

In

In writing the following work, I aim at perspicuity and simplicity of style; and try to avoid those unmeaning compliments, which slip from the tongue, but have not the least connexion with the affections that should warm the heart, and animate the conduct. By this false politeness, sincerity is sacrificed, and truth violated; and thus artificial manners are necessarily taught. For true politeness is a polish, not a varnish; and should rather be acquired by observation than admonition. And we may remark, by way of illustration, that men do not attempt to polish precious stones, till age and air have given them that degree of solidity, which will enable them to bear the necessary friction, without destroying the main substance.

The way to render instruction most useful cannot always be adopted; knowledge should be gradually imparted, and flow more from example than teaching: example directly addresses the senses,
the

the firſt inlets to the heart; and the improvement of thoſe inſtruments of the underſtanding is the object education ſhould have conſtantly in view, and over which we have moſt power. But to wiſh that parents would, themſelves, mould the ductile paſſions, is a chimerical wiſh, for the preſent generation have their own paſſions to combat with, and faſtidious pleaſures to purſue, neglecting thoſe pointed out by nature: we muſt therefore pour premature knowledge into the ſucceeding one; and, teaching virtue, explain the nature of vice. Cruel neceſſity!

The Converſations are intended to aſſiſt the teacher as well as the pupil; and this will obviate an objection which ſome may ſtart, that the ſentiments are not quite on a level with the capacity of a child. Every child requires a different mode of treatment; but a writer can only chooſe one, and

that

it muſt be modified by thoſe who
are actually engaged with young
people in their ſtudies.

The tendency of the reaſoning
obviouſly tends to fix principles of
truth and humanity on a ſolid and
ſimple foundation; and to make
religion an active, invigorating di-
rector of the affections, and not
a mere attention to forms. Syſ-
tems of Theology may be com-
plicated, but when the character
of the Supreme Being is diſplayed,
and He is recogniſed as the Uni-
verſal Father, the Author and
Centre of Good, a child may be
led to comprehend that dignity
and happineſs muſt ariſe from
imitating Him; and this conviction ſhould be twiſted into—
and be the foundation of every
inculcated duty.

At any rate, the Tales, which
were written to illuſtrate the moral, may recall it, when the mind
has gained ſufficient ſtrength to
diſcuſs the argument from which it
was deduced.   I N T R O-

INTRODUCTION.

MARY and Caroline, though the children of wealthy parents were, in their infancy, left entirely to the management of fervants, or people equally ignorant. Their mother died fuddenly, and their father, who found them very troublefome at home, placed them under the tuition of a woman of tendernefs and difcernment, a near relation, who was induced to take on herfelf the important charge through motives of compaffion.

They were fhamefully ignorant, confidering that Mary had been fourteen, and Caroline twelve years in the world. If they had been merely ignorant, the tafk would not have appeared fo arduous; but
they

they had caught every prejudice that the vulgar cafually inftill. In order to eradicate thefe prejudices, and fubftitute good habits inftead of thofe they had carelefsly contracted, Mrs. Mafon never fuffered them to be out of her fight. They were allowed to afk queftions on all occafions, a method fhe would not have adopted, had fhe educated them from the firft, according to the fuggeftions of her own reafon, to which experience had given its fanction.

They had tolerable capacities; but Mary had a turn for ridicule, and Caroline was vain of her perfon. She was, indeed, very handfome, and the inconfiderate encomiums that had, in her prefence, been lavifhed on her beauty made her, even at that early age, affected.

CON-

CONTENTS.

CHAP.

CONTENTS.

CHAP. VIII.

CHAP. IX.

CHAP. X.

CHAP. XI.

CHAP. XII.

CHAP. XIII

CHAP.

CONTENTS.

CHAP.

C O N T E N T S.

MORAL

MORAL CONVERSATIONS

AND

STORIES.

CHAP. I.

*The treatment of animals—The ant—
The bee—Goodness—The lark's nest
—The asses.*

ONE fine morning in spring,
some time after Mary and Caroline were settled in their new abode,
Mrs. Mason proposed a walk before
breakfast, a custom she wished to teach
imperceptibly, by rendering it amusing.

The sun had scarcely dispelled the
dew that hung on every blade of grass,
and filled the half-shut flowers; every
prospect smiled, and the freshness of

B   the

the air conveyed the moſt pleaſing ſen-
ſations to Mrs. Maſon's mind; but the
children were regardleſs of the ſur-
rounding beauties, and ran eagerly
after ſome inſects to deſtroy them.
Mrs. Maſon ſilently obſerved their
cruel ſports, without appearing to do
it; but ſtepping ſuddenly out of the
foot-path into the long graſs, her
buckle was caught in it, and ſtriving
to diſentangle herſelf, ſhe wet her feet;
which the children knew ſhe wiſhed
to avoid, as ſhe had been lately ſick.
This circumſtance rouſed their attention; and they forgot their amuſement
to enquire *why* ſhe had left the path;
and Mary could hardly reſtrain a laugh,
when ſhe was informed that it was
to avoid treading on ſome ſnails that
were creeping acroſs the narrow foot-
way. Surely, ſaid Mary, you do not
think there is any harm in killing a
ſnail, or any of thoſe naſty creatures
that crawl on the ground? I hate
them,

them, and fhould fcream if one was
to find its way from my clothes to
my neck ! With great gravity, Mrs.
Mafon afked how fhe dared to kill
any thing, unlefs it were to prevent
its hurting her ? Then, refuming a
fmiling face, fhe faid, Your education
has been neglected, my child; as we
walk along attend to what I fay, and
make the beft anfwers you can; and
do you, Caroline, join in the converfation.

You have already heard that God
created the world, and every inhabi-
tant of it. He is then called the Father of all creatures; and all are made
to be happy, whom a good and wife
God has created. He made thofe
fnails you defpife, and caterpillars, and
fpiders; and when he made them, did
not leave them to perifh, but placed
them where the food that is moft proper to nourifh them is eafily found. They
do not live long, but He who is their

Father,

Father, as well as your's, directs them
to deposit their eggs on the plants that
are fit to support their young, when
they are not able to get food for themselves.—And when such a great and
wise Being has taken care to provide
every thing necessary for the meanest
creature, would you dare to kill it,
merely because it appears to you
ugly? Mary began to be attentive,
and quickly followed Mrs. Mason's
example, who allowed a caterpillar
and a spider to creep on her hand.
You find them, she rejoined, very
harmless; but a great number would
destroy our vegetables and fruit; so
birds are permitted to eat them, as
we feed on animals; and in spring
there are always more than at any
other season of the year, to furnish food
for the young broods.—Half-con-
vinced, Mary said, but worms are of
little consequence in the world. Yet,
replied Mrs. Mason, God cares for
them,

them, and gives them every thing that is neceſſary to render their exiſt-ence comfortable. You are often troubleſome—I am ſtronger than you—yet I do not kill you.

Obſerve thoſe ants ; they have a little habitation in yonder hillock ; they carry food to it for their young, and ſleep very ſnug in it during the cold weather. The bees alſo have com-fortable towns, and lay up a ſtore of honey to ſupport them when the flowers die, and ſnow covers the ground : and this forecaſt is as much the gift of God, as any quality you poſſeſs.

Do you know the meaning of the word Goodneſs ? I ſee you are unwill-ing to anſwer. I will tell you. It is, firſt, to avoid hurting any thing ; and then, to contrive to give as much pleaſure as you can. If ſome inſects are to be deſtroyed, to preſerve my garden from deſolation, I have it done in the quickeſt way. The domeſtic

B 3   animals

animals that I keep, I provide the beſt
food for, and never ſuffer them to be
tormented ; and this caution ariſes
from two motives :—I wiſh to make
them happy ; and, as I love my fellow-
creatures ſtill better than the brute
creation, I would not allow thoſe that I
have any influence over, to grow habitually thoughtleſs and cruel, till they
were unable to reliſh the greateſt pleaſure life affords,—that of reſembling
God, by doing good.

A lark now began to ſing, as it ſoared
aloft. The children watched its motions, liſtening to the artleſs melody.
They wondered what it was thinking
of—of its young family, they ſoon concluded ; for it flew over the hedge,
and drawing near, they heard the young
ones chirp. Very ſoon both the old
birds took their flight together, to look
for food to ſatisfy the craving of the almoſt fledged young. An idle boy, who
had borrowed a gun, fired at them—

they

they fell; and before he could take up
the wounded pair, he perceived Mrs.
Mafon; and expecting a very fevere
reprimand, ran away. She and the
little girls drew near, and found that
one was not much hurt; but that the
other, the cock, had one leg broken,
and both its wings fhattered; and its
little eyes feemed ftarting out of their
fockets, it was in fuch exquifite pain.
The children turned away their eyes.
Look at it, faid Mrs. Mafon; do you
not fee that it fuffers as much, and
more than you did when you had the
fmall-pox, when you were fo tenderly
nurfed. Take up the hen; I will
bind her wing together; perhaps it
may heal. As to the cock, though I
hate to kill any thing, I muft put him
out of pain; to leave him in his prefent ftate would be cruel; and avoiding
an unpleafant fenfation myfelf, I fhould
allow the poor bird to die by inches,
and call this treatment tendernefs,

B 4   when

when it would be felfifhnefs or weaknefs. Saying fo, fhe put her foot on
the bird's head, turning her own another way.

They walked on; when Caroline
remarked, that the neftlings, deprived
of their parents, would now perifh;
and the mother began to flutter in her
hand as they drew near the hedge,
though the poor creature could not
fly, yet fhe tried to do it. The girls,
with one voice, begged Mrs. Mafon
to let them take the neft, and provide
food in a cage, and fee if the mother
could not contrive to hop about to
feed them. The neft and the old
mother were inftantly in Mary's hand-
kerchief. A little opening was left to
admit the air; and Caroline peeped
into it every moment to fee how they
looked. I give you leave, faid Mrs.
Mafon, to take thofe birds, becaufe
an accident has rendered them helplefs;

if

if that had not been the cafe, they fhould not have been confined.

They had fcarcely reached the next field, when they met another boy with a neft in his hand, and on a tree near him faw the mother, who, forgetting her natural timidity, followed the fpoiler; and her intelligible tones of anguifh reached the ears of the children, whofe hearts now firft felt the emotions of humanity. Caroline called him, and taking fixpence out of her little purfe, offered to give it to him for the neft, if he would fhew her where he had taken it from. The boy confented, and away ran Caroline to replace it,— crying all the way, how delighted the old bird will be to find her brood again. The pleafure that the parent-bird would feel was talked of till they came to a large common, and heard fome young affes, at the door of an hovel, making a moft dreadful noife. Mrs. Mafon had ordered the old ones to be con-

fined,

fined, left the young fhould fuck before the neceffary quantity had been
faved for fome fick people in her
neighbourhood. But after they had
given the ufual quantity of milk, the
thoughtlefs boy had left them ftill in
confinement, and the young in vain
implored the food nature defigned for
their particular fupport. Open the
hatch, faid Mrs. Mafon, the mothers
have ftill enough left to fatisfy their
young. It was opened, and they faw
them fuck.

Now, faid fhe, we will return to
breakfaft; give me your hands, my
little girls, you have done good this
morning, you have acted like rational
creatures. Look, what a fine morning
it is. Infects, birds, and animals, are
all enjoying this fweet day. Thank
God for permitting you to fee it, and
for giving you an underftanding which
teaches you that you ought, by doing
good, to imitate Him. Other creatures

tures only think of supporting themselves; but man is allowed to ennoble
his nature, by cultivating his mind and
enlarging his heart. He feels difinterefted love; every part of the creation affords an exercife for virtue, and
virtue is ever the trueft fource of
pleafure.

CHAP. II.

*The treatment of animals—The diffe-
rence between them and man—Parental affection of a dog—Brutality
punifhed.*

AFTER breakfaft, Mrs. Mafon
gave the children *Mrs. Trimmer's
Fabulous Hiftories*; and the fubject
ftill turned on animals, and the wan-
ton cruelty of thofe who treated them
improperly. The little girls were

eager

eager to expreſs their deteſtation, and requeſted that in future they might be allowed to feed the chickens. Mrs. Maſon complied with their requeſt; only one condition was annexed to the permiſſion, that they did it regularly. When you wait for your food, you learn patience, ſhe added, and you can mention your wants; but thoſe helpleſs creatures cannot complain. The country people frequently ſay,— How can you treat a poor dumb beaſt ill; and a ſtreſs is very properly laid on the word dumb;—for dumb they appear to thoſe who do not obſerve their looks and geſtures; but God, who takes care of every thing, under-ſtands their language; and ſo did Caroline this morning, when ſhe ran with ſuch eagerneſs to re-place the neſt which the thoughtleſs boy had ſtolen, heedleſs of the mother's ago-nizing cries!

Mary

Mary interrupted her, to afk, if infects and animals were not inferior to men; Certainly, anfwered Mrs. Mafon; and men are inferior to angels; yet we have reafon to believe, that thofe exalted beings delight to do us good. You have heard in a book, which I feldom permit you to read, becaufe you are not of an age to underftand it, that angels, when they fang glory to God on high, wifhed for peace on earth, as a proof of the good will they felt towards men. And all the glad tidings that have been fent to men, angels have proclaimed: indeed, the word angel fignifies a meffenger. In order to pleafe God, and our happinefs depends upon pleafing him, we muft do good. What we call virtue, may be thus explained:— we exercife every benevolent affection to enjoy comfort here, and to fit ourfelves to be angels hereafter. And when we have acquired human virtues,

we

we shall have a nobler employment in our Father's kingdom. But between angels and men a much greater resemblance subsists, than between men and the brute creation; because the two former seem capable of improvement.

The birds you saw to-day do not improve—or their improvement only tends to self-preservation; the first nest they make and the last are exactly the same; though in their flights they must see many others more beautiful if not more convenient, and,-had they reason, they would probably shew something like individual taste in the form of their dwellings; but this is not the case. You saw the hen tear the down from her breast to make a nest for her eggs; you saw her beat the grain with her bill, and not swallow a bit, till the young were satisfied; and afterwards she covered them with her wings, and seemed perfectly happy, while

while she watched over her charge; if any one approached, she was ready to defend them, at the hazard of her life: yet, a fortnight hence, you will see the same hen drive the fledged chickens from the corn, and forget the fondness that seemed to be stronger than the first impulse of nature.

Animals have not the affections which arise from reason, nor can they do good, or acquire virtue: Every affection, and impulse, which I have observed in them, are like our inferior emotions, which do not depend entirely on our will, but are involuntary; they seem to have been implanted to preserve the species, and make the individual grateful for actual kindness. If you caress and feed them, they will love you, as children do, without knowing why; but we neither see imagination nor wisdom in them; and, what principally exalts man, friendship and devotion, they seem incapable

incapable of forming the leaſt idea of. Friendſhip is founded on knowledge and virtue, and theſe are human acquirements; and devotion is a preparation for eternity; becauſe when we pray to God, we offer an affront to him, if we do not ſtrive to imitate the perfections He diſplays every where for our imitation, that we may grow better and happier.

The children eagerly enquired in what manner they were to behave, to prove that they were ſuperior to animals? The anſwer was ſhort,—be tender-hearted; and let your ſuperior endowments ward off the evils which they cannot foreſee. It is only to animals that children *can* do good, men are their ſuperiors. When I was a child, added their tender friend, I always made it my ſtudy and delight, to feed all the dumb family that ſurrounded our houſe; and when I could be of uſe to any one of them I was happy.

happy. This employment humanized my heart, while, like wax, it took every impreſſion; and Providence has ſince made me an inſtrument of good —I have been uſeful to my fellow-creatures. I, who never wantonly trod on an inſect, or diſregarded the plaint of the ſpeechleſs beaſt, can now give bread to the hungry, phyſic to the ſick, comfort to the afflicted, and, above all, am preparing you, who are to live for ever, to be fit for the ſociety of angels, and good men made perfect. This world, I told you, was a road to a better—a preparation for it; if we ſuffer, we grow humbler and wiſer: but animals have not this advantage, and man ſhould not prevent their enjoying all the happineſs of which they are capable.

A ſhe-cat or dog have ſuch ſtrong parental affection, that if you take away their young, it almoſt kills them; ſome have actually died of grief when

all

all have been taken away; though they do not seem to miss the greatest part.

A bitch had once all her litter stolen from her, and drowned in a neighbouring brook: she sought them out, and brought them one by one, laid them at the feet of her cruel master;—and looking wistfully at them for some time, in dumb anguish, turning her eyes on the destroyer, she expired!

I myself knew a man who had hardened his heart to such a degree, that he found pleasure in tormenting every creature whom he had any power over. I saw him let two guinea-pigs roll down sloping tiles, to see if the fall would kill them. And were they killed? cried Caroline. Certainly; and it is well they were, or he would have found some other mode of torment. When he became a father, he not only neglected to educate his children, and set them a good example,

but

but he taught them to be cruel while he tormented them : the confequence was, that they neglected him when he was old and feeble; and he died in a ditch.

You may now go and feed your birds, and tie fome of the ftraggling flowers round the garden fticks. After dinner, if the weather continues fine, we will walk to the wood, and I will fhew you the hole in the lime-ftone mountain (a mountain whofe bowels, as we call them, are lime-ftones) in which poor crazy Robin and his dog lived.

C H A P. III.

The treatment of animals—The ftory of crazy Robin—The man confined in the Baftille.

IN the afternoon the children bounded over the fhort grafs of the common, and

and walked under the fhadow of the mountain till they came to a craggy part; where a ftream broke out, and ran down the declivity, ftruggling with the huge ftones which impeded its progrefs, and occafioned a noife that did not unpleafantly interrupt the folemn filence of the place. The brook was foon loft in a neighbouring wood, and the children turned their eyes to the broken fide of the mountain, over which ivy grew in great profufion. Mrs. Mafon pointed out a little cave, and defired them to fit down on fome ftumps of trees, whilft fhe related the promifed ftory.

In yonder cave once lived a poor man, who generally went by the name of crazy Robin. In his youth he was very induftrious, and married my father's dairy-maid; a girl deferving of fuch a good hufband. For fome time they continued to live very comfortably; their daily labour procured their

daily

daily bread; but Robin, finding it was likely he ſhould have a large family, borrowèd a trifle, to add to the ſmall pittance which they had ſaved in ſervice, and took a little farm in a neighbouring county. I was then a child.

Ten or twelve years after, I heard that a crazy man, who appeared very harmleſs, had piled by the ſide of the brook a great number of ſtones; he would wade into the river for them, followed by a cur dog, whom he would frequently call his Jacky, and even his Nancy; and then mumble to himſelf,—thou wilt not leave me—we will dwell with the owls in the ivy.— A number of owls had taken ſhelter in it. The ſtones which he waded for he carried to the mouth of the hole, and only juſt left room enough to creep in. Some of the neighbours at laſt recollefted his face; and I ſent to enquire what misfortune had reduced him to ſuch a deplorable ſtate.

The

The information I received from different perfons, I will communicate to you in as few words as I can.

Several of his children died in their infancy; and, two years before he came to his native place, one misfortune had followed another till he had funk under their accumulated weight. Through various accidents he was long in arrears to his landlord; who, feeing that he was an honeft man, who endeavoured to bring up his family, did not diftrefs him; but when his wife was lying-in of her laft child, the landlord dying, his heir fent and feized the ftock for the rent; and the perfon from whom he had borrowed fome money, exafperated to fee all gone, arrefting him immediately, he was hurried to gaol, without being able to leave any money for his family. The poor woman could not fee them ftarve, and trying to fupport her children before fhe had gained fufficient

2   ftrength,

ſtrength, ſhe caught cold ; and through neglect, and her want of proper nouriſhment, her illneſs turned to a putrid fever; which two of the children caught from her, and died with her. The two who were left, Jacky and Nancy, went to their father, and took with them a cur dog, that had long ſhared their frugal meals.

The children begged in the day, and at night ſlept with their wretched father. Poverty and dirt ſoon robbed their cheeks of the roſes which the country air made bloom with a peculiar freſhneſs ; ſo that they ſoon caught a jail fever,—and died. The poor father, who was now bereft of all his children, hung over their bed in ſpeechleſs anguiſh; not a groan or a tear eſcaped from him, whilſt he ſtood, two or three hours, in the ſame attitude, looking at the dead bodies of his little darlings. The dog licked his hands, and ſtrove to attract his attention ;

attention; but for awhile he seemed
not to obscrve his caresses; when he
did, he said, mournfully, thou wilt
not leave me—and then he began to
laugh. The bodies were removed;
and he remained in an unsettled state,
often frantic; at length the phrenzy
subfided, and he grew melancholy and
harmless. He was not then so closely
watched; and one day he contrived
to make his escape, the dog followed
him, and came directly to his native
village.

After I had received this account,
I determined he should live in the
place he had chosen, undisturbed. I
sent some conveniences, all of which
he rejected, except a mat; on which
he sometimes slept—the dog always
did. I tried to induce him to eat,
but he constantly gave the dog whatever I sent him, and lived on haws
and blackberries, and every kind of
trash. I used to call frequently on
him :

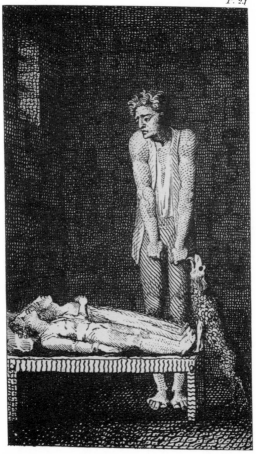

The Dog strove to attract his attention. —
He said. Thou wilt not leave me !

Published by J. Johnson, Sept.r 1, 1791.

him; and he sometimes followed me to the house I now live in, and in winter he would come of his own accord, and take a crust of bread. He gathered water-cresses out of the pool, and would bring them to me, with nosegays of wild thyme, which he plucked from the sides of the mountain. I mentioned before, that the dog was a cur. It had, indeed, the bad trick of a cur, and would run barking after horses heels. One day, when his master was gathering water-cresses, the dog running after a young gentleman's horse, made it start, and almost threw the rider; who grew so angry, that though he knew it was the poor madman's dog, he levelled his gun at his head—shot him,—and instantly rode off. Robin ran to his dog,—he looked at his wounds, and not sensible that he was dead, called to him to follow him; but when he found that he could not, he took him to the

C   pool,

pool, and waſhed off the blood before it began to clot, and then brought
him home, and laid him on the mat.

I obſerved that I had not ſeen him
pacing up the hills as uſual, and ſent
to enquire about him. He was found
ſitting by the dog, and no entreaties
could prevail on him to quit the body,
or receive any refreſhment. I in-
ſtantly ſet off for this place, hoping,
as I had always been a favourite, that
I ſhould be able to perſuade him to
eat ſomething. But when I came to
him, I found the hand of death was
upon him. He was ſtill melancholy;
yet there was not ſuch a mixture of
wildneſs in it as formerly. I preſſed
him to take ſome food; but, inſtead
of anſwering me, or turning away, he
burſt into tears,—a thing I had never
ſeen him do before, and, ſobbing, he
ſaid, Will any one be kind to me!
—you will kill me!—I ſaw not my
wife die—No!—they dragged me from
her

2

her—but I saw Jacky and Nancy die—
and who pitied me?—but my dog!
He turned his eyes to the body—I
wept with him. He would then have
taken some nourishment, but nature
was exhausted—and he expired.—

Was that the cave? said Mary.
They ran to it. Poor Robin! Did
you ever hear of any thing so cruel?
Yes, answered Mrs. Mason; and as
we walk home I will relate an instance
of still greater barbarity.

I told you, that Robin was confined
in a jail. In France they have a
dreadful one, called the Bastille. The
poor wretches who are confined in it
live entirely alone; have not the pleasure of seeing men or animals; nor
are they allowed books.—They live
in comfortless solitude. Some have
amused themselves by making figures
on the wall; and others have laid
straws in rows. One miserable cap-
tive found a spider; he nourished it

C 2

for

for two or three years; it grew tame, and partook of his lonely meal. The keeper obferved it, and mentioned the circumftance to a fuperiour, who ordered him to crufh it. In vain did the man beg to have his fpider fpared. You find, Mary, that the nafty creature which you defpifed was a com· fort in folitude. The keeper obeyed the cruel command; and the unhappy wretch felt more pain when he heard the crufh, than he had ever experienced during his long confinement. He looked round a dreary apartment, and the fmall portion of light which the grated bars admitted, only ferved to fhew him, that he breathed where nothing elfe drew breath.

CHAP.

CHAP. IV.

Anger.—History of Jane Fretful.

A Few days after thefe walks and converfations, Mrs. Mafon heard a great noife in the play-room. She ran haftily to enquire the caufe, and found the children crying, and near them, one of the young birds lying on the floor dead. With great eagernefs each of them tried, the moment fhe entered, to exculpate herfelf, and prove that the other had killed the bird. Mrs. Mafon commanded them to be filent; and, at the fame time, called an orphan whom fhe had educated, and defired her to take care of the neft.

The caufe of the difpute was eafily gathered from what they both let fall. They had contefted which had the beft right to feed the birds. Mary infifted

that

that fhe had a right, becaufe fhe was
the eldeft; and Caroline, becaufe fhe
took the neft. Snatching it from one
fide of the room to the other, the bird
fell, and was trodden on before they
were aware.

When they were a little compofed,
Mrs. Mafon calmly thus addreffed
them :—I perceive that you are a-
fhamed of your behaviour, and forry
for the confequence; I will not therefore feverely reprove you, nor add
bitternefs to the felf-reproach you
muft both feel,—becaufe I pity you.
You are now inferiour to the animals
that graze on the common; reafon
only ferves to render your folly more
confpicupus and inexcufable. Anger,
is a little defpicable vice : its felfifh
emotions banifh compaffion, and undermine every virtue. It is eafy to
conquer another ; but noble to fubdue
onefelf. Had you, Mary, given
way to your fifter's humour, you would
have proved that you were not only
older,

older, but wifer than her. And you, Caroline, would have faved your charge, if you had, for the time, waved your right.

It is always a proof of fuperiour fenfe to bear with flight inconveniences, and even trifling injuries, without complaining or contefting about them. The foul referves its firmnefs for great occafions, and then it acts a decided part. It is juft the contrary mode of thinking, and the conduct produced by it, which occafions all thofe trivial difputes that flowly corrode domeftic peace, and infenfibly deftroy what great misfortunes could not fweep away.

I will tell you a ftory, that will take ftronger hold on your memory than mere remarks.

Jane Fretful was an only child. Her fond weak mother would not allow her to be contradicted on any occafion. The child had fome tendernefs of heart;

C 4 but

but so accustomed was she to see every thing give way to her humour, that she imagined the world was only made for her. If any of her playfellows had toys, that struck her capricious sickly fancy, she would cry for them; and substitutes were in vain offered to quiet her, she must have the identical ones, or fly into the most violent passion. When she was an infant, if she fell down, her nurse made her beat the floor. She continued the practice afterwards, and when she was angry would kick the chairs and tables, or any senseless piece of furniture, if they came in her way. I have seen her throw her cap into the fire, because some of her acquaintance had a prettier.

Continual passions weakened her constitution; beside, she would not eat the common wholesome food that children, who are subject to the small-pox and worms, ought to eat, and which is necessary when they grow so

fast,

faft, to make them ftrong and handfome. Inftead of being a comfort to
her tender, though miftaken, mother,
fhe was her greateft torment. The
fervants all difliked her; fhe loved no
one but herfelf; and the confequence
was, fhe never infpired love; even
the pity good-natured people felt, was
nearly allied to contempt.

A lady, who vifited her mother,
brought with her one day a pretty little
dog. Jane was delighted with it; and the
lady, with great reluctance, parted with
it to oblige her friend. For fome time
fhe fondled, and really felt fomething
like an affection for it: but, one day,
it happened to fnatch a cake fhe was
going to eat, and though there were
twenty within reach, fhe flew into a violent paffion, and threw a ftool at the
poor creature, who was big with pup.
It fell down; I can fcarcely tell the
reft; it received fo fevere a blow, that
all the young were killed, and the poor

C 5   wretch

wretch languished two days, suffering the most excruciating torture.

Jane Fretful, who was now angry with herself, sat all the time holding it, and every look the miserable animal gave her, stung her to the heart. After its death she was very unhappy; but did not try to conquer her temper. All the blessings of life were thrown away on her; and, without any real misfortune, she was continually miserable.

If she had planned a party of pleasure, and the weather proved unfavourable, the whole day was spent in fruitless repining, or venting her ill-humour on those who depended on her. If no disappointment of that kind occurred, she could not enjoy the promised pleasure; something always disconcerted her; the horses went too fast, or, too slow; the dinner was ill-dressed, or, some of the company contradicted her.

She was, when a child, very beautiful; but anger soon distorted her regular

gular features, and gave a forbidding
fierceneſs to her eyes. But if for a
moment ſhe looked pleaſed, ſhe ſtill
reſembled a heap of combuſtible matter, to which an accidental ſpark
might ſet fire; of courſe quiet people
were afraid to converſe with her.
And if ſhe ever did a good, or a humane action, her ridiculous anger ſoon
rendered it an intolerable burden, if
it did not entirely cancel it.

At laſt ſhe broke her mother's heart,
or haſtened her death, by her want of
duty, and her many other faults: all
proceeding from violent, unreſtrained
anger.

The death of her mother, which
affected her very much, left her without a friend. She would ſometimes
ſay, Ah! my poor mother, if you
were now alive, I would not teaze you
—I would give the world to let you
know that I am ſorry for what I have
done: you died, thinking me ungrate-

ful;

ful; and lamenting that I did not die when you gave me fuck. I fhall never—oh! never fee you more.

This thought, and her peevifh temper, preyed on her impaired conftitution. She had not, by doing good, prepared her foul for another ftate, or cherifhed any hopes that could difarm death of its terrors, or render that laft fleep fweet—its approach was dreadful!—and fhe haftened her end, fcolding the phyfician for not curing her. Her lifelefs countenance difplayed the marks of convulfive anger; and fhe left an ample fortune behind her to thofe who did not regret her lofs. They followed her to the grave, on which no one fhed a tear. She was foon forgotten; and I only remember her, to warn you to fhun her errors.

CHAP.

CHAP. V.

Lying—Honor—Truth—Small Duties —Hiſtory of Lady Sly, and Mrs. Trueman.

THE little girls were very aſſidu-ous to gain Mrs. Maſon's good opinion ; and, by the mildneſs of their behaviour, to prove to her that they were aſhamed of themſelves. It was one of Mrs. Maſon's rules, when they offended her, that is, behaved impro-perly, to treat them civilly ; but to avoid giving them thoſe marks of af-fection which they were particularly delighted to receive.

Yeſterday, ſaid ſhe to them, I only mentioned to you one fault, though I obſerved two. You very readily gueſs I mean the lie that you both told. Nay, look up, for I wiſh to ſee you bluſh ; and the confuſion which I per-ceive in your faces gives me pleaſure ; becauſe it convinces me that it is not

a cona confirmed habit: and, indeed, my children, I should be sorry that such a mean one had taken deep root in your infant minds.

When I speak of falsehood, I mean every kind; whatever tends to deceive, though not said in direct terms. Tones of voice, motions of the hand or head, if they make another believe what they ought not to believe, are lies, and of the worst kind; because the contrivance aggravates the guilt. I would much sooner forgive a lie told directly, when perhaps fear entirely occupied the thoughts, and the presence of God was not felt: for it is His sacred Majesty that you affront by telling an untruth.

How so? enquired Mary.

Because you hope to conceal your falsehood from every human creature: but, if you consider a moment, you must recollect, that the Searcher of hearts reads your very thoughts; that nothing is hid from him.

You

You would blush if I were to discover that you told a lie; yet wantonly forfeit the favour of Him, from whom you have received life and all its blessings, to screen yourselves from correction or reproof, or, what is still worse, to purchase some trifling gratification, the pleasure of which would last but a moment.

You heard the gentleman who visited me this morning, very frequently use the word Honour. Honour consists in respecting yourself; in doing as you would be done by; and the foundation of honour is Truth.

When I can depend on the veracity of people, that is to say, am convinced that they adhere to truth, I rely on them; am certain they have courage, because I know they will bear any inconvenience rather than despise themselves, for telling a lie. Besides, it is not necessary to consider what you intend to say, when you have done right. Always determine, on every occasion, to speak the truth, and you will never be at a loss for words. If your character for this scrupulous attention is once fixed, your acquaintance will be courted; and those who are not particularly pleased with you, will, at least, respect your honourable principles..

It is impossible to form a friendship without making truth the basis; it is indeed the essence of devotion, the employment of the understanding, and the support of every duty.

I govern my servants, and you, by attending strictly to truth, and this observance keeping my head clear and my heart pure, I am ever ready to pray to the Author of good, the Fountain of truth.

While I am discussing the subject, let me point out to you another branch of this virtue; Sincerity —And remember that I every day set you an example; for I never, to please for the moment, pay unmeaning compliments,

or

or permit any words to drop from my tongue, that my heart does not dictate. And when I relate any matter of fact, I carefully avoid embellishing it, in order to render it a more entertaining story; not that I think such a practice absolutely criminal; but as it contributes insensibly to wear away a respect for truth, I guard against the vain impulse, lest I should lose the chief strength, and even ornament, of my mind, and become like a wave of the sea, drifted about by every gust of passion.

You must in life observe the most apparently insignificant duties — the great ones are the pillars of virtue; but the constant concurrence of trifling things, makes it necessary that reason and conscience should always preside, to keep the heart steady. Many people make promises, and appointments, which they scruple not to break, if a more inviting pleasure occurs, not

remem-

remembering that the flighteft duty
fhould be performed before a mere
amufement is purfued—for any neglect
of this kind embitters play. Nothing,
believe me, can long be pleafant, that
is not innocent.

As I ufually endeavour to recollect fome perfons of my acquaintance,
who have fuffered by the faults, or
follies, I wifh you to avoid; I will
defcribe two characters, that will, if
I miftake not, very ftrongly enforce
what I have been faying.

Laft week you faw Lady Sly, who
came to pay me a morning vifit. Did
you ever fee fuch a fine carriage, or
fuch beautiful horfes? How they pawed
the ground, and difplayed their rich
harneffes! Her fervants wore elegant
liveries, and her own clothes fuited the
equipage. Her houfe is equal to her
carriage; the rooms are lofty, and
hung with filk; noble glaffes and pictures adorn them: and the pleafure-
grounds

grounds are large and well laid out; beside the trees and shrubs, they contain a variety of summer-houses and temples, as they are called.—Yet my young friends, this is *state*, not *dignity*.

This woman has a little soul, she never attended to truth, and obtaining great part of her fortune by falsehood, it has blighted all her enjoyments. She inhabits that superb house, wears the gayest clothes, and rides in that beautiful carriage, without feeling pleasure. Suspicion, and the cares it has given birth to, have wrinkled her countenance, and banished every trace of beauty, which paint in vain endeavours to repair. Her suspicious temper arises from a knowledge of her own heart, and the want of rational employments.

She imagines that every person she converses with means to deceive her; and when she leaves a company, supposes all the ill they may say of her, because becaufe fhe recollects her own practice. She liftens about her houfe, expecting to difcover the defigns of her fer-vants, none of whom fhe can truft; and in confequence of this anxiety her fleep is unfound, and her food taftelefs. She walks in her paradife of a garden, and fmells not the flowers, nor do the birds infpire her with cheerfulnefs.—Thefe pleafures are true and fimple, they lead to the love of God, and all the creatures whom He hath made—and cannot warm a heart which a malicious ftory can pleafe.

She cannot pray to God ;—He hates a liar! She is neglected by her hufband, whofe only motive for marrying her was to clear an incumbered eftate. Her fon, her only child, is undutiful ; the poor never have caufe to blefs her ; nor does fhe contribute to the happi-nefs of any human being.

To

To kill time, and drive away the pangs of remorse, she goes from one house to another, collecting and propagating scandalous tales, to bring others on a level with herself. Even those who resemble her are afraid of her; she lives alone in the world, its good things are poisoned by her vices, and neither inspire joy nor gratitude.

Before I tell you how she acquired these vicious habits, and enlarged her fortune by disregarding truth, I must desire you to think of Mrs. Trueman, the curate's wife, who lives in yonder white house, close to the church; it is a small one, yet the woodbines and jessamins that twine about the windows give it a pretty appearance. Her voice is sweet, her manners not only easy, but elegant; and her simple dress makes her person appear to the greatest advantage.

She walks to visit me, and her little ones hang on her hands, and cling to
her

her clothes, they are so fond of her. If any thing terrifies them, they run under her apron, and she looks like the hen taking care of her young brood. The domestic animals play with the children, finding her a mild attentive mistress; and out of her scanty fortune she contrives to feed and clothe many a hungry shivering wretch; who bless her as she passes along.

Though she has not any outward decorations, she appears superior to her neighbours, who call her the *Gentlewoman*; indeed every gesture shews an accomplished and dignified mind, that relies on itself; when deprived of the fortune which contributed to polish and give it consequence.

Drawings, the amusement of her youth, ornament her neat parlour; some musical instruments stand in one corner; for she plays with taste, and sings sweetly.

All

All the furniture, not forgetting a book-cafe, full of well-chofen books, fpeak the refinement of the owner, and the pleafures a cultivated mind has within its own grafp, independent of profperity.

Her hufband, a man of tafte and learning, reads to her, while fhe makes clothes for her children, whom fhe teaches in the tendereft, and moft per-fuafive manner, important truths and elegant accomplifhments.

When you have behaved well for fome time you fhall vifit her, and ramble in her little garden; there are feveral pretty feats in it, and the nightingales warble their fweeteft fongs, undifturbed, in the fhade.

I have now given you an account of the prefent fituation of both, and of their characters; liften to me whilft I relate in what manner thefe characters were formed, and the confequence of each adhering to a different mode of conduct.

Lady

Lady Sly, when she was a child, used to say pert things, which the injudicious people about her laughed at, and called very witty. Finding that her prattle pleased, she talked incessantly, and invented stories, when adding to those that had some foundation, was not sufficient to entertain the company. If she stole sweetmeats, or broke any thing, the cat, or the dog, was blamed, and the poor animals were corrected for her faults; nay, sometimes the servants lost their places in consequence of her assertions. Her parents died and left her a large fortune, and an aunt, who had a still larger, adopted her.

Mrs. Trueman, her cousin, was, some years after, adopted by the same lady; but her parents could not leave their estate to her, as it descended to the male heir. She had received the most liberal education, and was in every respect the reverse of her cousin; who

envied

envied her merit, and could not bear to think of her dividing the fortune which she had long expected to inherit entirely herself. She therefore practised every mean art to prejudice her aunt against her, and succeeded.

A faithful old servant endeavoured to open her mistress's eyes; but the cunning niece contrived to invent the most infamous story of the old domestic, who was in consequence of it dismissed. Mrs. Trueman supported her, when she could not succeed in vindicating her, and suffered for her generosity; for her aunt dying soon after, left only five hundred pounds to this amiable woman, and fifty thousand to Lady Sly.

They both of them married shortly after. One, the profligate Lord Sly, and the other a respectable clergyman, who had been disappointed in his hopes of preferment. This last couple, in spite of their mutual disappointments, are contented with their lot; and are preparing themselves and children for

D   another

another world, where truth, virtue and happiness dwell together.

For believe me, whatever happiness we attain in this life, muſt faintly reſemble what God Himſelf enjoys, whoſe truth and goodneſs produce a ſublime degree, ſuch as we cannot conceive, it is ſo far above our limited capacities.

I did not intend to detain you ſo long, ſaid Mrs. Maſon; have you finiſhed *Mrs. Trimmer's Fabulous Hiſtories?* Indeed we have, anſwered Caroline, mournfully, and I was very ſorry to come to the end. I never read ſuch a pretty book; may I read it over again to Mrs. Trueman's little Fanny? Certainly, ſaid Mrs. Maſon, if you can make her underſtand that birds never talk. Go and run about the garden, and remember the next lie I detect, I ſhall puniſh; becauſe lying is a vice;—and I ought to puniſh you if you are guilty of it, to prevent your feeling Lady Sly's miſery.

CHAP.

C H A P. VI.

*Anger — Folly produces Self-contempt,
and the Neglect of others.*

MRS. Mason had a number of
visitors one afternoon, who conversed in the usual thoughtless manner
which people often fall into who do
not consider before they speak; they
talked of Caroline's beauty, and she
gave herself many affected airs to
make it appear to the best advantage.
But Mary, who had not a face to be
proud of, was observing some pecu-
liarities in the dress or manners of
the guests; and one very respectable
old lady, who had lost her teeth, afforded her more diversion than any of
the rest.

The children went to bed without
being reproved, though Mrs. Mason,
when she dismissed them, said gravely,

I give

I give you to-night a kifs of peace,
an affectionate one you have not deferved. They therefore difcovered
by her behaviour that they had done
wrong, and waited for an explanation
to regain her favour.

She was never in a paffion, but her
quiet fteady difpleafure made them feel
fo little in their own eyes, they wifhed
her to fmile that they might be fomething; for all their confequence feemed
to arife from her approbation. I declare,
faid Caroline, I do not know what I
have done, and yet I am fure I never
knew Mrs. Mafon find fault without
convincing me that I had done wrong.
Did you, Mary, ever fee her in a
paffion? No, faid Mary, I do believe that fhe was never angry in her
life; when John threw down all the
china, and ftood trembling, fhe was
the firft to fay that the carpet made
him ftumble. Yes, now I do remember, when we firft came to her
houfe, John forgot to bring the cow
and

and her young calf into the cow-
house; I heard her bid him do it directly, and the poor calf was almost
frozen to death—she spoke then in a
hurry, and seemed angry: Now you
mention it, I do recollect, replied Caroline, that she was angry, when Betty
did not carry the poor sick woman the
broth she ordered her to take to her.
But this is not like the passion I used
to see nurse in, when any thing vexed
her. She would scold us, and beat the
girl who waited on her. Poor little
Jenny, many a time was she beaten,
when we vexed nurse; I would tell her
she was to blame now if I saw her
— and I would not tease her any
more.

I declare I cannot go to sleep, said
Mary, I am afraid of Mrs. Mason's
eyes—would you think, Caroline, that
she who looks so very good-natured
sometimes, could frighten one so? I
wish I were as wise and as good as
she is. The poor woman with the

D 3   six

six children, whom we met on the common, said she was an angel, and that she
had saved her's and her children's
lives. My heart is in my mouth,
indeed, replied Caroline, when I think
of to-morrow morning, and yet I am
much happier than I was when we
were at home. I cried, I cannot now
tell for what, all day; I never wished
to be good—nobody told me what
it was to be good. I wish to be a
woman, said Mary, and to be like
Mrs. Mason, or Mrs. Trueman,—we
are to go to see her if we behave well.

Sleep soon over-powered them, and
they forgot their apprehensions. In
the morning they awoke refreshed,
and took care to learn their lessons,
and feed the chickens, before Mrs.
Mason left her chamber.

C H A P.

C H A P. VII.

*Virtue the Soul of Beauty—The Tulip
and the Rose—The Nightingale—
External Ornaments—Characters.*

THE next morning Mrs. Ma-
son met them first in the garden; and she desired Caroline to look
at a bed of tulips, that were then
in their highest state of perfection. I,
added she, choose to have every kind
of flower in my garden, as the succes-
sion enables me to vary my daily
prospect, and gives it the charm of
variety; yet these tulips afford me less
pleasure than most of the other sort
which I cultivate—and I will tell you
why—they are only beautiful. Listen
to my distinction; — good features,
and a fine complexion, I term *bodily*
beauty. Like the streaks in the tulip, they please the eye for a moment;

D 4 but

but this uniformity soon tires, and the active mind flies off to something else. The soul of beauty, my dear children, consists in the body gracefully exhibiting the emotions and variations of the informing mind. If truth, humanity, and knowledge inhabit the breast, the eyes will beam with a mild lustre, modesty will suffuse the cheeks, and smiles of innocent joy play over all the features. At first sight, regularity and colour will attract, and have the advantage, because the hidden springs are not directly set in motion; but when internal goodness is reflected, every other kind of beauty, the shadow of it, withers away before it—as the sun obscures a lamp.

You are certainly handsome, Caroline; I mean, have good features; but you must improve your mind to give them a pleasing expression, or they will only serve to lead your understanding astray. I have seen
some

some foolish people take great pains
to decorate the outside of their houses,
to attract the notice of strangers, who
gazed, and passed on; whilst the in-
side, where they received their friends,
was dark and inconvenient. Apply
this observation to mere personal at-
tractions. They may, it is true, for a few
years, charm the superficial part of your
acquaintance, whose notions of beauty
are not built on any principle of
utility. Such persons might look at
you, as they would glance their eye
over these tulips, and feel for a moment the same pleasure that a view
of the variegated rays of light would
convey to an uninformed mind. The
lower class of mankind, and children,
are fond of finery; gaudy, dazzling
appearances catch their attention; but
the discriminating judgment of a person of sense requires, besides colour,
order, proportion, grace and useful-
ness, to render the idea of beauty
complete.

Observe

Obferve that rofe, it has all the perfections I fpeak of; colour, grace, and fweetnefs—and even when the fine tints fade, the fmell is grateful to thofe who have before contemplated its beauties. I have only one bed of tulips, though my garden is large, but, in every part of it, rofes attract the eye.

You have feen Mrs. Trueman, and think her a very fine woman; yet her fkin and complexion have only the clearnefs that temperance gives; and her features, ftrictly fpeaking, are not regular : Betty, the houfe-maid, has, in both thefe refpects, much the fuperiority over her. But, though it is not eafy to define in what her beauty confifts, the eye follows her whenever fhe moves; and every perfon of tafte liftens for the modulated founds which proceed out of her mouth, to be improved and pleafed. It is confcious worth, *truth*, that gives dignity to her walk, and fimple elegance to her conver-

converfation. She has, indeed, a moft
excellent underftanding, and a feeling heart; fagacity and tendernefs,
the refult of both, are happily blend-
ed in her countenance; and tafte is
the polifh, which makes them appear
to the beft advantage. She is more
than beautiful; and you fee her varied excellencies again and again, with
increafing pleafure. They are not
obtruded on you, for knowledge has
taught her true humility: fhe is not
like the flaunting tulip, that forces
itfelf forward into notice; but refembles the modeft rofe, you fee
yonder, retiring under its elegant
foliage.

I have mentioned flowers — the
fame order is obferved in the higher
departments of nature. Think of the
birds; thofe that fing beft have not
the fineft plumage; indeed juft the
contrary; God divides His gifts, and
amongft the feathered race the nightingale (fweeteft of warblers, who
pours

pours forth her varied strain when
sober eve comes on) you would seek
in vain in the morning, if you expected that beautiful feathers should
point out the songstress: many who
incessantly twitter, and are only tolerable in the general concert, would
surpass her, and attract your attention.

I knew, some time before you were
born, a very fine, a very handsome
girl; I saw she had abilities, and I
saw with pain that she attended to
the most obvious, but least valuable
gift of heaven. Her ingenuity slept,
whilst she tried to render her person more alluring. At last she caught
the small-pox—her beauty vanished,
and she was for a time miserable;
but the natural vivacity of youth over-
came her unpleasant feelings. In
consequence of the disorder, her eyes
became so weak that she was obliged
to sit in a dark room. To beguile
the tedious day she applied to music,

2   and

and made a furprifing proficiency. She even began to think, in her retirement, and when fhe recovered her fight grew fond of reading.

Large companies did not now amufe her, fhe was no longer the object of admiration, or if fhe was taken notice of, it was to be pitied, to hear her former felf praifed, and to hear them lament the depredation that dreadful difeafe had made in a fine face. Not expecting or wifhing to be obferved, fhe loft her affected airs, and attended to the converfation, in which fhe was foon able to bear a part. In fhort, the defire of pleafing took a different turn, and as fhe improved her mind, fhe difcovered that virtue, internal beauty, was valuable on its own ac-count, and not like that of the perfon, which refembles a toy, that pleafes the obferver, but does not render the poffeffor happy.

She found, that in acquiring know-ledge, her mind grew tranquil, and the
noble

noble defire of acting conformably to the will of God fucceeded, and drove out the immoderate vanity which before actuated her, when her equals were the objects fhe thought moft of, and whofe approbation fhe fought with fuch eagernefs. And what had fhe fought? To be ftared at and called handfome. Her beauty, the mere fight of it, did not make others good, or comfort the afflicted; but after fhe had loft it, fhe was comfortable herfelf, and fet her friends the moft ufeful example.

The money that fhe had formerly appropriated to ornament her perfon, now clothed the naked; yet fhe really appeared better dreffed, as fhe had acquired the habit of employing her time to the beft advantage, and could make many things herfelf. Befides, fhe did not implicitly follow the reigning fafhion, for fhe had learned to diftinguifh, and in the moft trivial mat-

ters

ters acted according to the dictates of good sense.

The children made some comments on this story, but the entrance of a visitor interrupted the conversation, and they ran about the garden, comparing the roses and tulips.

CHAP. VIII.

Summer Evening's Amusement.—The Arrival of a Family of Haymakers.— Ridicule of personal Defects censured. —A Storm.—The Fear of Death.— The Cottage of honest Jack, the ship-wrecked Sailor.—The History of Jack, and his faithful Dog Pompey.

THE evening was pleasant; Mrs. Mason and the children walked out; and many rustic noises struck their ears. Some bells in a neighbouring village, softened by the distance, sounded pleasingly; the beetles hummed,

med, and the children purfued them,
not to deftroy them; but to obferve
their form, and afk queftions concern-
ing their mode of living. Sheep were
bleating and cattle lowing, the rivulet
near them babbled along, while the
found of the diftant ocean died away
on the ear—or they forgot it, liftening
to the whiftling of the hay-makers,
who were returning from the field.
They met a whole family who came
every year from another county where
they could not find conftant employment, and Mrs. Mafon allowed them
to fleep in her barn. The little ones
knew their benefactrefs, and tried to
catch a fmile; and fhe was ever ready
to fmile on thofe whom fhe obliged;
for fhe loved all her fellow creatures,
and love lightens obligations. Befides,
fhe thought that the poor who are willing to work, had a right to the comforts of life.

A few moments after, they met a
deformed woman; the children ftared

her

her almoſt out of countenance; but
Mrs. Maſon turned her head another
way, and when the poor object was
out of hearing, ſaid to Mary, I intended to reprove you this morning
for a fault which I have frequently
ſeen you commit; and this moment
and the other evening it was particularly conſpicuous. When that deformed
woman paſſed us, I involuntarily looked
at ſomething elſe, and would not let
her perceive that ſhe was a diſguſting
figure, and attracted notice on that
account. I ſay I did it involuntarily,
for I have accuſtomed myſelf to think
of others, and what they will ſuffer
on all occaſions: and this lothneſs to
offend, or even to hurt the feelings
of another, is an inſtantaneous ſpring
which actuates my conduct, and makes
me kindly affected to every thing that
breathes. If I then am ſo careful not
to wound a ſtranger, what ſhall I think
of your behaviour, Mary? when you
laughed at a reſpectable old woman,
who

who befide her virtues and her age,
had been particularly civil to you. I
have always feen perfons of the weakeft
underftandings, and whofe hearts benevolence feldom touched, ridicule bodily infirmities, and accidental defects.
They could only relifh the inferiour
kind of beauty, which I defcribed this
morning, and a filly joy has elated
their empty fouls, on finding, by com-
parifon, that they were fuperiour to
others in that refpect, though the con-
clufion was erroneous, for merit, men-
tal acquirements, can only give a juft
claim to fuperiority. Had you poffeffed the fmalleft portion of difcernment, you would foon have forgotten the tones, lofs of teeth made draw-
ling, in liftening to the chearful good
fenfe which that worthy woman's words
conveyed. You laughed, becaufe you
were ignorant, and I now excufe
you; but fome years hence, if I were
to fee you in company, with fuch a
propenfity, I fhould ftill think you
a child,

a child, an overgrown one, whofe mind did not expand as the body grew.

The fky began to thicken, and the lowing of the cattle to have a melancholy cadence; the nightingale forgot her fong, and fled to her neft; and the fea roared and lafhed the rocks. During the calm which portended an approaching ftorm, every creature was running for fhelter.—We muft, if poffible, faid Mrs. Mafon, reach yon cottage on the cliff, for we fhall foon have a violent thunder-ftorm. They quickened their pace, but the hurricane overtook them. The hail-ftones fell, the clouds feemed to open and difclofe the lightning, while loud peals of thunder fhook the ground; the wind alfo in violent gufts rufhed among the trees, tore off the flender branches and loofened the roots.

The children were terrified; but Mrs Mafon gave them each a hand, and chatted with them to difpel their fears. She informed them that ftorms were

neceffary

neceffary to diffipate noxious vapours,
and to anfwer many other purpofes,
which were not, perhaps, obvious to
our weak underftandings. But are
you not afraid? cried the trembling
Caroline. No, certainly, I am not
afraid.—I walk with the fame fecurity
as when the fun enlivened the profpect
—God is ftill prefent, and we are fafe.
Should the flafh that paffes by us,
ftrike me dead, it cannot hurt me, I
fear not death!—I only fear that Being
who can render death terrible, on
whofe providence I calmly reft; and
my confidence earthly forrows cannot
deftroy. A mind is never truly great,
till the love of virtue overcomes the
fear of death.

By this time they had mounted the
cliff, and faw the tumultuous deep.
The angry billows rofe, and dafhed
againft the fhore; and the loud noife
of the raging fea refounded from rock
to rock.

They

They ran into the cottage; the poor woman who lived in it, fent her children for wood, and foon made a good fire to dry them.

The father of the family foon after came in, leaning on crutches; and over one eye there was a large patch. I am glad to fee you honeft Jack, faid Mrs. Mafon, come and take your feat by the fire, and tell the children the ftory of your fhipwreck.

He inftantly complied. I was very young, my dear ladies, faid Jack, when I went to fea, and endured many hardfhips,—however I made a fhift to weather them all; and whether the wind was fair or foul, I ran up the fhrouds and fung at the helm. I had always a good heart, no lad fore or aft had a better; when we were at fea, I never was the firft to flinch; and on fhore I was as merry as the beft of them. I married fhe you fee yonder, (lifting his crutch to point to his wife) and her work and my wages did

did together, till I was shipwrecked on these rocks. Oh! it was a dreadful night; this is nothing to it; but I am getting to the end of my story before I begin it.

During the war, I went once or twice to New York. The last was a good voyage, and we were all returning with joy to dear England, when the storm rose; the vessel was like a bird, it flew up and down, and several of our best hands were washed clean overboard—My poor captain! a better never plowed the ocean, he fell overboard too, and it was some time before we missed him; for it was quite dark, except that flashes of lightning, now and then, gave us light. I was at the helm, lashing it to the side of the ship—a dreadful flash came across me, and I lost one of my precious eyes.—But thank God I have one left.

The weather cleared up next day, and, though we had been finely mauled, I began to hope, for I hate to be faint-

4   hearted,

hearted, and certainly we fhould have got into the channel very foon, if we had not fell in with a French man of war, which took us; for we could not make any refiftance.

I had a dog, poor Pompey! with me. Pompey would not leave me, he was as fond of me as if he had been a chriftian. I had loft one eye by the lightning, the other had been fore, fo that I could hardly call it a peep-hole. Somehow I fell down the hatch-way, and bruifed one of my legs; but I did not mind it, do ye fee, till we arrived at Breft and were thrown into a French Prifon.

There I was worfe off than ever; the room we were all ftowed in, was full of vermin, and our food very bad; mouldy bifcuits, and falt fifh. The prifon was choke full, and many a morning did we find fome honeft fellow with his chops fallen—he was not to be waked any more!—he was gone to the other country, do ye fee.

Yet

Yet the French have not such hard hearts as people say they have! Several women brought us broth, and wine; and one gave me some rags to wrap round my leg, it was very painful, I could not clean it, nor had I any plaister. One day I was looking sorrowfully at it, thinking for certain I should lose my precious limb; when, would you believe it? Pompey saw what I was thinking about, and began to lick it.—And, I never knew such a surprizing thing, it grew better and better every day, and at last was healed without any plaister.

After that I was very sick, and the same tender-hearted creature who gave me the rags, took me to her house; and fresh air soon recovered me. I for certain ought to speak well of the French; but for their kindness I should have been in another port by this time. Mayhap I might have gone with a fair wind, yet I should have been sorry to have

have left my poor wife and her children. But I am letting all my line
run out! Well, by-and-by, there was
an exchange of prisoners, and we were
once more in an English vessel, and
I made sure of seeing my family
again; but the weather was still
foul. Three days and nights we were
in the greatest distress; and the fourth
the ship was dashed against these rocks.
Oh! if you had heard the crash!
The water rushed in — the men
screamed, Lord have mercy on us!
There was a woman in the ship, and,
as I could swim, I tried to save
her, and Pompey followed me; but
I lost him—poor fellow! I declare I
cried like a child when I saw his dead
body. However I brought the woman
to shore; and assisted some more of my
mess-mates; but, standing in the water so long, I lost the use of my
limbs—yet Heaven was good to me;
Madam, there, sent a cart for us all,
and took care of us; but I never

L.   reco-

recovered the use of my limbs. So she asked me all about my misfortunes, and sent for wife, who came directly, and we have lived here ever since. We catch fish for Madam, and I watch for a storm, hoping some time or other to be as kind to a poor perishing soul as she has been to me. Indeed we are very happy— I might now have been begging about the streets, but for Madam, God bless her.

A tear strayed down Mrs. Mason's cheek, while a smile of benevolence lighted up her countenance—the little girls caught each hand—They were all silent a few minutes when she, willing to turn the discourse, enquired whether they had any fish in the house? Some were produced, they were quickly dressed, and they all eat together. They had a chearful meal, and honest Jack sung some of his seafaring songs, and did all he could to divert them and express his gratitude.

Indeed we are very happy !————

Published by J. Johnson, Sept.ʳ 1, 1791.

titude. Getting up to reach the brown loaf, he limped very awkwardly, Mary was just beginning to laugh, when she restrained herself; for she recollected that his awkwardness made him truly respectable, because he had lost the use of his limbs when he was doing good, saving the lives of his fellow-creatures.

The weather cleared up, and they returned home. The children conversed gaily with each other all the way home, talking of the poor sailor, and his faithful dog.

CHAP. IX.

The Inconveniences of immoderate Indulgence.

THE children were allowed to help themselves to fruit, when it made a part of their meal; and Caroline always took care to pick out

the

the beſt, or ſwallow what ſhe took
in a hurry, leſt ſhe ſhould not get
as much as ſhe wiſhed for. Indeed
ſhe generally eat more than her ſhare.
She had ſeveral times eaten more
than a perſon ought to eat at one
time, without feeling any ill effects;
but one afternoon ſhe complained of
a pain in her ſtomach in conſequence
of it, and her pale face, and languid
eyes, plainly ſhewed her indiſpoſition.
Mrs. Maſon gave her an emetic,
and after the operation ſhe was
obliged to go to bed, though ſhe
had promiſed herſelf a pleaſant walk
that evening. She was left alone,
for Mary was not permitted to ſtay
at home with her, as ſhe offered to
do. Had her ſickneſs been accidental, we would both have tried to
amuſe her, ſaid Mrs. Maſon; but her
greedineſs now receiving its natural
and juſt puniſhment, ſhe muſt endure
it without the alleviation which pity
affords; only tell her from me, that
the

the pleaſure was but momentary, while the pain and confinement it produced, has already laſted ſome hours.

The next morning, though ſcarcely recovered, ſhe got up, as uſual, to have a walk before breakfaſt. During theſe walks, Mrs. Maſon told them ſtories, pointed out the wiſdom of God in the creation, and took them to viſit her poor tenants. Theſe viſits not only enabled her to form a judgment of their wants, but made them very induſtrious; for they were all anxious that ſhe might find their houſes and perſons clean. And returning through the farm-yard, Mrs. Maſon ſtopped according to cuſtom, to ſee whether the poor animals were taken care of—this ſhe called earning her breakfaſt. The ſervant was juſt feeding the pigs, and though ſhe poured a great quantity into the trough, the greedy creatures tried to gobble it up from one another. Ca-

E 3   roline

roline blufhed, fhe faw this fight was meant for her, and fhe felt afhamed of her gluttony. But Mrs. Mafon, willing to imprefs her ftill more ftrongly, thus addreffed her.

Providence, my child, has given us paffions and appetites for various purpofes—two are generally obvious, I will point them out to you. Firft to render our prefent life more comfortable, and then to prepare us for another, by making us fociable beings; as in fociety virtue is acquired, and felf-denial practifed. A moderate quantity of proper food recruits our exhaufted fpirits, and invigorates the animal functions; but, if we exceed moderation, the mind will be oppreffed, and foon become the flave of the body, or both grow liftlefs and inactive. Employed various ways, families meet at meals, and there giving up to each other, learn in the moft eafy, pleafant way to govern their appetites. Pigs, you

fee

fee, devour what they can get; but men, if they have any affections, love their fellow-creatures, and wish for a return; nor will they, for the fake of a brutish gratification, lofe the esteem of thofe they value. Befides, no one can be reckoned virtuous who has not learned to bear poverty: yet thofe who think much of gratifying their appetites, will at laft act meanly in order to indulge them. But when any employment of the underftanding, or ftrong affection occupies the mind, eating is feldom thought a matter of greater importance than it ought to be. Let the idle *think* of their meals; but do you employ the intermediate time in a different manner, and only enjoy them when you join the focial circle. I like to fee children, and even men, eat chearfully, and gratefully receive the bleffings fent by Heaven; yet I would not have them abufe thofe bleffings, or ever let the care

neceffary

neceffary to fupport the body, injure
the immortal fpirit: many think of
the fuftenance the former craves, and
entirely neglect the latter.

I remarked to you before, that
in the moft apparently trivial con-
cerns, we are to do as we would
be done by. This duty muft be
practifed conftantly; at meals there
are frequent opportunities, and I hope,
Caroline, I fhall never again fee
you eager to fecure dainties for
yourfelf. If fuch a difpofition were
to grow up with you, you ought to
live alone, for no one fhould enjoy
the advantages and pleafures which
arife from focial intercourfe, who is
unwilling to give way to the incli-
nations of others, and allow each
their fhare of the good things of this
life.

You experienced yefterday, that
pain follows immoderate indulgence;
it is always the cafe, though fometimes not felt fo immediately; but
the

the conftitution is infenfibly deftroyed, and old age will come on, loaded with infirmities. You alfo loft a very pleafant walk, and fome fine fruit. We vifited Mrs. Goodwin's garden, and as Mary had before convinced me that fhe could regulate her appetites, I gave her leave to pluck as much fruit as fhe wifhed; and fhe did not abufe my indulgence. On the contrary, fhe fpent moft part of the time in gathering fome for me, and her attention made it tafte fweeter.

Coming home I called her my friend, and fhe deferved the name, for fhe was no longer a child; a reafonable affection had conquered an appetite; her underftanding took the lead, and fhe had practifed a virtue.

The fubject was now dropped; but, Caroline determined to copy in future her fifter's temperance and felf-denial.

E 5   C H A P.

C H A P. X.

The Danger of Delay—Description of a Mansion-house in Ruins—The History of Charles Townley.

MRS. Mason who always regulated her own time, and never loitered her hours irresolutely away, had very frequently to wait for the children, when she wished to walk, though she had desired them to be ready at a precise time. Mary in particular had a trick of putting every thing off till the last moment, and then she did but half do it, or left it undone. This indolent way of delaying made her miss many opportunities of obliging and doing good; and whole hours were lost in thoughtless idleness, which she afterwards wished had been better employed.

This

This was the cafe one day, when
fhe had a letter to write to her father; and though it was mentioned
to her early in the morning, the
fineft part of the evening flipped away
whilft fhe was finifhing it; and her
hafte made her forget the principal
thing which fhe intended to have faid.

Out of breath fhe joined them;
and after they had croffed feveral
fields, Mrs. Mafon turning down a
long avenue, bade them look at a large
old manfion-houfe. It was now in
ruins. Ivy grew over the fubftantial
walls, that ftill refifted the depre-
dations of time, and almoft concealed
a noble arch, on which maimed lions
couched; and vultures. and eagles,
who had loft their wings, feemed to
reft for ever there. Near it was a
rookery, and the rooks lived fafe in
the high trees, whofe trunks were all
covered with ivy or mofs, and a number of funguffes grew about their
large roots. The grafs was long,

and

and remaining undisturbed, save when the wind swept acrofs it, was of courfe pathlefs. Here the mower never whet his scythe, nor did the haymakers mix their songs with the hoarse croaking of the rooks. A spacious basin, on the margin of which water plants grew with wild-luxuriance, was overspread with slime; and afforded a shelter for toads and adders. In many places were heaped the ruins of ornamental buildings, whilst sun-dials rested in the shade;—and pedestals that had crushed the figures they before supported. Making their way through the grass, they would frequently stumble over a headless statue, or the head would impede their progrefs. When they spoke, the sound seemed to return again, as if unable to penetrate the thick stagnated air. The sun could not dart its purifying rays through the thick gloom, and the fallen leaves contributed to choke up the way, and render the air more noxious.

I brought

I brought you to this place on pur-
pofe this evening, faid Mrs. Mafon to
the children, who clung about her, to
tell you the hiftory of the laft inhabit-
ant; but, as this part is unwholefome,
we will fit on the broken ftones of
the drawbridge.

Charles Townley was a boy of uncommon abilities, and ftrong feelings;
but he ever permitted thofe feelings to
direct his conduct, without fubmitting
to the direction of reafon; I mean, the
prefent emotion governed him.—He
had not any ftrength or confiftency of
character; one moment he enjoyed a
pleafure, and the next felt the pangs of
remorfe, on account of fome duty
which he had neglected. He always
indeed intended to act right in every
particular *to-morrow*; but *to-day* he
followed the prevailing whim.

He heard by chance of a man in
great diftrefs, he determined to relieve
him, and left his houfe in order to follow the humane impulfe; but meeting
an

an acquaintance, he was perfuaded to go to the play, and *to-morrow*, he thought, he would do the act of charity. The next morning fome company came to breakfaft with him, and took him with them to view fome fine pictures. In the evening he went to a concert; the day following he was tired, and laid in bed till noon; then read a pathetic ftory, well wrought up, *wept* over it—fell afleep—and forgot to *act* humanely. An accident reminded him of his intention, he fent to the man, and found that he had too long delayed—the relief was ufelefs.

In this thoughtlefs manner he fpent his time and fortune; never applying to any profeffion, though formed to fhine in any one he fhould have chofen. His friends were offended, and at laft allowed him to languifh in a gaol; and as there appeared no probability of reforming or fixing him, they left him to ftruggle with adverfity.

Severely

Severely did he reproach himfelf—He was almost lost in despair, when a friend vifited him. This friend loved the latent sparks of virtue which he imagined would some time or other light up, and animate his conduct. He paid his debts, and gave him a sum of money sufficient to enable him to prepare for a voyage to the East Indies, where Charles wished to go, to try to regain his lost fortune. Through the interceffion of this kind, considerate friend, his relations were reconciled to him, and his spirits raised.

He sailed with a fair wind, and fortune favouring his most romantic wishes, in the space of fifteen years, he acquired a much larger fortune than he had even hoped for, and thought of vifiting, nay, settling in his native country for the remainder of his life.

Though impreffed by the most lively sense of gratitude, he had dropped his friend's correspondence; yet, as he knew that he had a daughter, his first

determination

determination was to referve for her the greater part of his property, as the moft fubftantial proof which he could give of his gratitude.——The thought pleafed him, and that was fufficient to divert him for fome months; but accidentally hearing that his friend had been very unfuccefsful in trade, this information made him wifh to haften his return to his native country. Still a procraftinating fpirit poffeffed him, and he delayed from time to time the arduous tafk of fettling his affairs, previous to his departure: he wrote, however, to England, and tranfmitted a confiderable fum to a correfpondent, defiring that this houfe might be prepared for him, and the mortgage cleared.

I can fcarcely enumerate the various delays that prevented his embarking; and when he arrived in England, he came here, and was fo childifhly eager to have his houfe fitted up with tafte, that he actually trifled away a month, before he went to feek for his friend.

2   But

But his negligence was now severely punished. He learned that he had been reduced to great diſtreſs, and thrown into the very gaol, out of which he took Townley, who, haſtening to it, only found his dead body there; for he died the day before. On the table was lying, amidſt ſome other ſcraps of paper, a letter, directed in an unſteady hand to Charles Townley. He tore it open. Few were the ſcarcely legible lines; but they ſmote his heart. He read as follows:

" I have been reduced by unfore-
" ſeen misfortunes; yet when I heard
" of your arrival, a gleam of joy
" cheered my heart—*I thought I knew
" your's*, and that my latter days
" might ſtill have been made com-
" fortable in your ſociety, for I loved
" you; I even expected pleaſure; but
" I was miſtaken; death is my only
" friend."

He

He read it over and over again; and cried out, Gracious God, had I arrived but one day fooner I fhould have feen him, and he would not have died thinking me the moſt ungrateful wretch that ever burdened the earth! He then knocked his clinched fiſt againſt his forehead, looked wildly round the dreary apartment, and exclaimed in a choked, though impatient tone, You fat here yeſterday, thinking of my ingratitude—Where are you now! Oh! that I had feen you! Oh! that my repenting fighs could reach you!—

He ordered the body to be interred, and returned home a prey to grief and defpondency. Indulging it to excefs, he neglected to enquire after his friend's daughter; he intended to provide amply for her, but now he could only grieve.

Some time elapfed, then he fent, and the intelligence which he procured

aggra-

aggravated his diftrefs, and gave it a
fevere additional fting.

The poor gentle girl had, during
her father's life, been engaged to a
worthy young man; but, fome time
after his death, the relations of her
lover had fent him to fea to prevent the
match taking place. She was helplefs, and had not fufficient courage
to combat with poverty; to efcape
from it, fhe married an old rake whom
fhe detefted. He was ill-humoured,
and his vicious habits rendered him
a moft dreadful companion. She tried
in vain to pleafe him, and banifh the
forrow that bent her down, and made
wealth and all the pleafures it could
procure taftelefs. Her tender father
was dead—fhe had loft her lover—
without a friend or confident, filent
grief confumed her. I have told you
friendfhip is only to be found amongft
the virtuous; her hufband was vicious.

Ah !

Ah! why did she marry, said Mary?

Becaufe she was timid; but I have not told you all; the grief that did not break her heart, difturbed her reafon; and her hufband confined her in a mad-houfe.

Charles heard of this laft circum-ftance; he vifited her. Fanny, faid he, do you recollect your old friend? Fanny looked at him, and reafon for a moment refumed her feat, and in-formed her countenance to trace an-guifh on it—the trembling light foon difappeared—wild fancy flufhed in her eyes, and animated her inceffant rant. She fung feveral verfes of different fongs, talked of her hufband's ill-ufage—enquired if he had lately been to fea? And frequently addreffed her father as if he were behind her chair, or fitting by her.

Charles could not bear this fcene—If I could lofe like her a fenfe of woe, he cried, this intolerable anguifh would

not

not tear my heart ! The fortune which he had intended for her could not reſtore her reaſon ; but, had he ſent for her ſoon after her father's death, he might have ſaved her and comforted himſelf.

The laſt ſtroke was worſe than the firſt ; he retired to this abode ; melancholy creeping on him, he let his beard grow, and the garden run wild. One room in the houſe the poor lunatic inhabited ; and he had a proper perſon to attend her, and guard her from the dangers ſhe wiſhed to encounter. Every day he viſited her, the ſight of her would almoſt have unhinged a ſound mind—How could he bear it, when his conſcience reproached him, and whiſpered that he had neglected to do good, to live to any rational purpoſe—The ſweets of friendſhip were denied, and he every day contemplated the ſaddeſt of all ſights—the wreck of a human underſtanding.

He

He died without a will. The estate was litigated, and as the title to this part could not be proved, the house was let fall into its present state.

But the night will overtake us, we must make haste home—Give me your hand, Mary, you tremble; surely I need not desire you to remember this story—Be calm, my child, and remember that you must attend to trifles; do all the good you can the present day, nay hour, if you would keep your conscience clear. This circumspection may not produce dazzling actions, nor will your silent virtue be supported by human applause; but your Father, who seeth in secret, will reward you.

CHAP.

*Be calm, my child, remember that you
must do all the good you can the present day.*

Published by J. Johnson, Sept.ʳ 1 1791.

CHAP. XI.

Dress. — A Character. — Remarks on Mrs. Trueman's Manner of dressing. Trifling Omissions undermine Affection.

MARY's procrastinating temper produced many other ill consequences; she would lie in bed till the last moment, and then appear without washing her face or cleaning her teeth. Mrs. Mason had often observed it, and hinted her dislike; but, unwilling to burden her with precepts, she waited for a glaring example. One was soon accidentally thrown in her way, and she determined that it should not pass unobserved.

A lady, who was remarkable for her negligence in this respect, spent a week with them; and, during that time, very frequently disconcerted the œconomy of the family. She was seldom

fit

fit to be feen, and if any company came by chance to dinner, fhe would make them wait till it was quite cold, whilft fhe huddled on fome ill-chofen finery. In the fame ftyle, if a little party of pleafure was pro-pofed, fhe had to drefs herfelf, and the hurry difcompofed her, and tired thofe, who did not like to lofe time in anticipating a trifling amufement.

A few hours after fhe had left them, Mrs. Mafon enquired of Mary, what effect this week's experience had had on her mind? You are fond of ridicule, child, but feldom in the right place; real caufe for it you let flip, and heed not the filent reproof that points at your own faults: do not miftake me, I would not have you laugh at—yet I wifh you to feel, what is ridiculous, and learn to dif-tinguifh folly. Mrs. Dowdy's neglig-ence arifes from indolence; her mind is not employed about matters of im-portance; and, if it were, it would not

be

be a sufficient excuse for her habitually neglecting an essential part of a man's as well as a woman's duty. I said habitually; grief will often make those careless, who, at other times, pay a proper attention to their person; and this neglect is a sure indication that the canker-worm is at work; and we ought to pity, rather than blame the unfortunate. Indeed when painful activity of mind occasions this inattention, it will not last long; the soul struggles to free itself, and return to its usual tone and old habits. The lady we have been speaking of, ever appears a sloven, though she is sometimes a disgusting figure, and, at others, a very taudry flirt.

I continually caution Caroline not to spend much time in adorning her person; but I never desired you to neglect yours. Wisdom consists in avoiding extremes—immoderate fondness for dress, I term vanity; but a proper attention to avoid singularity

F   does

does not deserve that name. Never waste much time about trifles; but the time that is necessary, employ properly. Exercise your understanding, taste flows from it, and will in a moment direct you, if you are not too solicitous to conform to the changing fashions; and loiter away in laborious idleness the precious moments when the imagination is most lively, and should be allowed to fix virtuous affections in the tender youthful heart.

Of all the women whom I have ever met with, Mrs. Trueman seems the freest from vanity, and those frivolous views which degrade the female character. Her virtues claim respect, and the practice of them engrosses her thoughts; yet her clothes are apparently well chosen, and you always see her in the same attire. Not like many women who are eager to set off their persons to the best advantage, when they are only going to take a walk, and are careless, nay slovenly, when forced

to

to stay at home. Mrs. Trueman's conduct is just the reverse, she tries to avoid singularity, for she does not wish to disgust the generality; but it is her family, her friends, whom she studies to please.

In dress it is not little minute things, but the *whole* that should be attended to, and that every day; and this attention gives an ease to the person because the clothes appear unstudily graceful. Never, continued Mrs. Mason, desire to excel in trifles, if you do——there is an end to virtuous emulation, the mind cannot attend to both; for when the main pursuit is trivial, the character will of course become insignificant. Habitual neatness is laudable; but, if you wish to be reckoned a well, an elegantly dressed girl; and feel that praise on account of it gives you pleasure, you are vain; and a laudable ambition cannot dwell with vanity.

Servants, and those women whose minds have had a very limited range, place all their happiness in ornaments,

and

and frequently neglect the only essential part in dress,—neatness.

I have not the least objection to your dressing according to your age; I rather encourage it, by allowing you to wear the gayest colours; yet I insist on some degree of uniformity: and think you treat me disrespectfully when you appear before me, and have forgotten to do, what should never be neglected, and what you could have done in less than a quarter of an hour.

I always dress myself before breakfast, and expect you to follow my example, if there is not a sufficient, and obvious excuse. You, Mary, missed a pleasant airing yesterday; for if you had not forgotten the respect which is due to me, and hurried down to breakfast in a slovenly manner, I should have taken you out with me; but I did not choose to wait till you were ready, as your not being so was entirely your own fault.

Fathers,

Fathers, and men in general, complain of this inattention; they have always to wait for females. Learn to avoid this fault, however infignificant it may appear in your eyes, for that habit cannot be of little confequence that fometimes weakens efteem. When we frequently make allowance for another in trifling matters, notions of inferiority take root in the mind, and too often produce contempt. Refpect for the underftanding muft be the bafis of conftancy; the tendernefs which flows from pity is liable to perifh infenfibly, to confume itfelf—even the virtues of the heart, when they degenerate into weaknefs, fink a character in our eftimation. Befides, a kind of grofs familiarity, takes place of decent affection; and the refpect which alone can render domeftic intimacy a lafting comfort is loft before we are aware of it.

F 3　　　　CHAP.

CHAP. XII.

*Behaviour to Servants.—True Dignity of
Character.*

THE children not coming down
to breakfast one morning at the
usual time, Mrs. Mason went herself
to enquire the reason; and as she entered the apartment, heard Mary say
to the maid who assisted her, I wonder
at your impertinence, to talk thus to
me—do you know who you are speaking to?—she was going on; but Mrs.
Mason interrupted her, and answered
the question—to a little girl, who is
only assisted because she is weak.
Mary shrunk back abashed, and Mrs.
Mason continued, as you have treated
Betty, who is ten years older than
yourself, improperly, you must now
do every thing for yourself; and, as
you will be some time about it,
Caroline and I will eat our breakfast,
and

and visit Mrs. Trueman. By the time we return, you may perhaps have recollected that children are inferior to servants—who act from the dictates of reason, and whose understandings are arrived at some degree of maturity, while children must be governed and directed till *their's* gains strength to work by itself: for it is the proper exercise of our reason that makes us in any degree independent.

When Mrs. Mason returned, she mildly addressed Mary. I have often told you that every dispensation of Providence tended to our improvement, if we do not perversely act contrary to our interest. One being is made dependent on another, that love and forbearance may soften the human heart, and that linked together by necessity, and the exercise of the social affections, the whole family on earth might have a fellow feeling for each other. By these means we improve

F 4   one

one another; but there is no real inferiority.

You have read the fable of the
head fuppofing itfelf fuperior to the
reft of the members, though all are
equally neceffary to the fupport of life.
If I behave improperly to fervants, I
am really their inferior, as I abufe a
truft, and imitate not the Being,
whofe fervant I am, without a fhadow
of equality. Children are helplefs. I
order my fervants to wait on you, becaufe you are fo; but I have not as
much refpect for you as for them;
you may poffibly become a virtuous
character.—Many of my fervants are
really fo already; they have done their
duty, filled an humble ftation, as they
ought to fill it, confcientioufly. And
do you dare to defpife thofe whom
your Creator approves?

Before the greateft earthly beings I
fhould not be awed, they are my fellow fervants; and, though fuperior in
rank, which, like perfonal beauty,
only

only dazzles the vulgar; yet I may possess more knowledge and virtue. The same feeling actuates me when I am in company with the poor; we are creatures of the same nature, and I may be their inferiour in those graces which should adorn my soul, and render me truly great.

How often must I repeat to you, that a child is inferiour to a man; because reason is in its infancy, and it is reason which exalts a man above a brute; and the cultivation of it raises the wise man above the ignorant; for wisdom is only another name for virtue.

This morning, when I entered your apartment, I heard you insult a worthy servant. You had just said your prayers; but they must have been only the gabble of the tongue; your heart was not engaged in the sacred employment, or you could not so soon have forgotten that you were a weak, dependent being, and that you were

F 5

to

to receive mercy and kindnefs only on the condition of your practifing the fame.

I advife you to afk Betty to pardon your impertinence; till you do fo, fhe fhall not affift you; you would find yourfelf very helplefs without the af-fiftance of men and women—unable to cook your meat, bake your bread, wafh your clothes, or even put them on—fuch a helplefs creature is a child —I know what you are, you per-ceive.

Mary fubmitted—and in future after fhe faid her prayers, remembered that fhe was to endeavour to curb her tem-per.

CHAP.

C H A P. XIII.

Employment—Idleness produces Misery—The Cultivation of the Fancy raises us above the Vulgar, extends our Happiness, and leads to Virtue.

ONE afternoon, Mrs. Mason gave the children leave to amuse themselves; but a kind of liftlessness hung over them, and at a loss what to do, they seemed fatigued with doing nothing. They eat cakes though they had juft dined, and did many foolish things merely becaufe they were idle. Their friend feeing that they were irrefolute, and could not fix on any employment, requefted Caroline to affift her to make fome clothes, that a poor woman was in want of, and while we are at work, fhe added, Mary will read us an entertaining tale, which I will point out.

F 6 The

The tale interested the children, who chearfully attended, and after it was finished, Mrs. Mason told them, that as she had some letters to write, she could not take her accustomed walk; but that she would allow them to reprefent her, and act for once like women. They received their commission, it was to take the clothes to the poor woman, whom they were intended for; learn her present wants; exercise their own judgment with respect to the immediate relief she stood in need of, and act accordingly.

They returned home delighted, eager to tell what they had done, and how thankful, and happy they had left the poor woman.

Observe now, said Mrs. Mason, the advantages arising from employment; three hours ago, you were uncomfortable, without being sensible of the cause, and knew not what to do with yourselves. Nay, you actually committed a sin; for you devoured cakes without feel-

2   ing

ing hunger, merely to kill time, whilſt many poor people have not the means of ſatisfying their natural wants. When I deſired you to read to me you were amuſed ; and now you have been uſeful you are delighted. Recollect this in future when you are at a loſs what to do with yourſelves—and remember that idleneſs muſt always be intolerable, becauſe it is only an irkſome conſciouſneſs of exiſtence.

Every gift of Heaven is lent to us for our improvement; fancy is one of the firſt of the inferiour ones ; in cultivating it, we acquire what is called taſte, or a reliſh for particular employments, which occupy our leiſure hours, and raiſe us above the vulgar in our converſation. Thoſe who have not any taſte talk always of their own affairs or of their neighbours ; every trivial matter that occurs within their knowledge they canvaſs and conjecture about—not ſo much out of ill-nature as idleneſs : juſt as you eat the cakes with-

out

out the impulfe of hunger. In the fame ftyle people talk of eating and drefs, and long for their meals merely to divide the day, becaufe the intermediate time is not employed in a more interefting manner. Every new branch of tafte that we cultivate, affords us a refuge from idlenefs, a fortrefs in which we may refift the affaults of vice; and the more noble our employments, the more exalted will our minds become.

Mufic, drawing, works of ufefulnefs and fancy, all amufe and refine the mind, fharpen the ingenuity; and form, infenfibly, the dawning judgment.—As the judgment gains ftrength, fo do the paffions alfo; we have actions to weigh, and need that tafte in conduct, that delicate fenfe of propriety, which gives grace to virtue. The higheft branch of folitary amufement is reading; but even in the choice of books the fancy is firft employed; for in reading, the heart is touched, till
its

its feelings are examined by the underftanding, and the ripenings of reafon
regulate the imagination. This is the
work of years, and the moft important
of all employments. When life ad-
vances, if the heart has been capable
of receiving early impreffions, and the
head of reafoning and retaining the
conclufions which were drawn from
them; we have acquired a ftock of
knowledge, a gold mine which we
can occafionally recur to, independent of outward circumftances.

The fupreme Being has every thing
in himfelf; we proceed from Him, and
our knowledge and affections muft
return to Him for employment fuited
to them. And thofe who moft refemble Him ought, next to Him, to
be the objects of our love; and the
beings whom we fhould try to af-
fociate with, that we may receive
an inferiour degree of fatisfaction from
their fociety. — But be affured our
chief comfort muft ever arife from
the

the mind's reviewing its own ope-
rations—and the whispers of an ap-
proving conscience, to convince us that
life has not slipped away unemployed.

CHAP. XIV.

*Innocent Amusements.—Description of
a Welsh Castle.—History of a Welsh
Harper.—A tyrannical Landlord.—
Family Pride.*

AS it was now harvest time, the
new scene, and the fine weather
delighted the children, who ran continually out to view the reapers. Indeed every thing seemed to wear a
face of festivity, and the ripe corn
bent under its own weight, or, more
erect, shewed the laughing appearance
of plenty.

Mrs. Mason always allowing the
gleaners to have a sufficient quantity,
a great

a great number of poor came to gather a little harveſt; and ſhe was pleaſed to ſee the feeble hands of childhood and age, collecting the ſcattered ears.

Honeſt Jack came with his family; and when the labours of the day were over, would play on a fiddle, that frequently had but three ſtrings. But it ſerved to ſet the feet in motion, and the lads and laſſes dancing on the green ſod, ſuffered every care to ſleep.

An old Welſh harper generally came to the houſe about this time of the year, and ſtaid a month or more; for Mrs. Maſon was particularly fond of this inſtrument, and intereſted in the fate of the player; as is almoſt always the caſe, when we have reſcued a perſon out of any diſtreſs.

She informed the children, that once travelling through Wales, her carriage was overturned near the ruins

of

of an old caftle. And as fhe had ef-
caped unhurt, fhe determined to wander
amongft them, whilft the driver took
care of his horfes, and her fervant
haftened to the neighbouring village
for affiftance.

It was almoft dark, and the lights began to twinkle in the fcattered cottages.
The fcene pleafed me, continued Mrs.
Mafon, I thought of the various cuftoms
which the lapfe of time unfolds; and
dwelt on the ftate of the Welfh, when
this caftle, now fo defolate, was the
hofpitable abode of the chief of a noble
family. Thefe reflections entirely en-
groffed my mind, when the found
of a harp reached my ears. Never
was any thing more opportune, the
national mufic feemed to give reality to
the pictures which my imagination had
been drawing. I liftened awhile, and
then trying to trace the pleafing found,
difcovered, after a fhort fearch, a
little hut, rudely built. The walls of
an old tower fupported part of the
thatch,

Trying to trace the sound, I discovered a little hut, rudely built.

Published by J. Johnson Sept.ʳ 1796.

thatch, which scarcely kept out the rain, and the two other sides were stones cemented, or rather plaistered together, by mud and clay.

I entered, and beheld an old man, sitting by a few loose sticks, which blazed on the hearth; and a young woman, with one child at her breast, sucking, and another on her knee: near them stood a cow and her calf. The man had been playing on the harp, he rose when he saw me, and offered his chair, the only one in the room, and sat down on a large chest in the chimney-corner. When the door was shut, all the light that was admitted came through the hole, called a chimney, and did not much enliven the dwelling. I mentioned my accident to account for my intrusion, and requested the harper again to touch the instrument that had attracted me. A partition of twigs and dried leaves divided this apartment from another, in which I perceived a light;

I enquired

I enquired about it, and the woman, in an artlefs manner, informed me, that fhe had let it to a young gentle-woman lately married, who was related to a very good family, and would not lodge any where, or with any body. This intelligence made me fmile, to think that family pride fhould be a folace in fuch extreme poverty.

I fat there fome ·time, and then the harper accompanied me to fee whether the carriage was repaired; I found it waiting for me; and as the inn I was to fleep at was only about two miles further, the harper offered to come and play to me whilft I was eating my fupper. This was juft what I wifhed for, his appearance had roufed my compaffion as well as my curiofity, and I took him and his harp in the chaife.

After fupper he informed me, that he had once a very good farm; but he had been fo unfortunate as to dif-pleafe the juftice, who never forgave him,

him, nor rested till he had ruined him. This tyrant always expected his tenants to assist him to bring in his harvest before they had got in their own. The poor harper was once in the midst of his, when an order was sent to him to bring his carts and servants, the next day, to the fields of this petty king. He foolishly refused; and this refusal was the foundation of that settled hatred which produced such fatal consequences. Ah, Madam, said the sufferer, your heart would ache, if you heard of all his cruelties to me, and the rest of his poor tenants. He employs many labourers, and will not give them as much wages as they could get from the common farmers, yet they dare not go any-where else to work when he sends for them. The fish that they catch they must bring first to him, or they would not be allowed to walk over his grounds to catch them; and he will give just

what

what he pleaſes for the moſt valuable part of their pannier.

But there would be no end to my ſtory were I to tell you of all his oppreſſions. I was obliged to leave my farm; and my daughter, whom you ſaw this evening, having married an induſtrious young man, I came to live with them. When,—would you believe it? this ſame man threw my ſon into jail, on account of his killing a hare, which all the country folks do when they can catch them in their grounds. We were again in great diſtreſs, and my daughter and I built the hut you ſaw in the waſte, that the poor babes might have a ſhelter. I maintain them by playing on the harp,—the maſter of this inn allows me to play to the gentry who travel this way; ſo that I pick up a few pence, juſt enough to keep life and ſoul together, and to enable me to ſend a little bread to my poor ſon John Thomas.

He then began one of the moſt diſmal of his Welſh ditties, and, in the midſt

of

of it cried out, he is an upſtart, a mere muſhroom!—His grandfather was cow-boy to mine!—So I told him once, and he never forgot it.—

The old man then informed me that the caſtle in which he now was ſhelter-ed formerly belonged to his family—ſuch are the changes and chances of this mortal life—ſaid he, and haſtily ſtruck up a lively tune.—

While he was ſtriking the ſtrings, I thought too of the changes in life which an age had produced. The deſcen-dant of thoſe who had made the hall ring with ſocial mirth now mourned in its ruins, and hung his harp on the mouldering battlements. Such is the fate of buildings and of families!

After I had diſmiſſed my gueſt, I ſent for the landlord, to make ſome farther enquiries; and found that I had not been deceived; I then determined to aſſiſt him, and thought my accident providential. I knew a man of conſe-quence in the neighbourhood, I viſited him,

4

him, and exerted myfelf to procure the enlargement of the young man. I fucceeded; and not only reftored him to his family; but prevailed on my friend to let him rent a fmall farm on his eftate, and I gave him money to buy ftock for it, and the implements of hufbandry.

The old harper's gratitude was unbounded; the fummer after he walked to vifit me; and ever fince he has contrived to come every year to enliven our harveft-home.—This evening it is to be celebrated.

The evening came; the joyous party footed it away merrily, and the found of their fhoes was heard on the barnfloor. It was not the light fantaftic toe, that fafhion taught to move, but honeft heart-felt mirth, and the loud laugh, if it fpoke the vacant head, faid audibly that the heart was guilelefs.

Mrs. Mafon always gave them fome trifling prefents at this time, to render the

the approach of winter more comfortable. To the men, fhe generally prefented warm clothing, and to the women flax and worfted for knitting and fpinning; and thofe who were the moft induftrious received a reward when the new year commenced. The children had books given to them, and little ornaments.—All were anxious for the day; and received their old acquaintance, the harper, with the moft cordial fmiles.

C H A P. XV.

Prayer.—A Moon-light Scene.— Refignation.

THE harper would frequently fit under a large elm, a few paces from the houfe, and play fome of the moft plaintive Welfh tunes. While the people were eating their fupper, Mrs. Mafon defired him to play her fome favourite airs; and fhe and the

G   children

children walked round the tree under which he fat, on the ftump of another.

The moon rofe in cloudlefs majefty, and a number of ftars twinkled near her. The foftened landfcape infpired tranquillity, while the ftrain of ruftic melody gave a pleafing melancholy to the whole—and made the tear ftart, whofe fource could fcarcely be traced. The pleafure the fight of harmlefs mirth gave rife to in Mrs. Mafon's bofom, roufed every tender feeling—fet in motion her fpirits.—She laughed with the poor whom fhe had made happy, and wept when fhe recollected her own forrows; the illufions of youth—the gay expectations that had formerly clipped the wings of time.— She turned to the girls—I have been very unfortunate, my young friends; but my griefs are now of a placid kind. Heavy misfortunes have obfcured the fun I gazed at when firft I entered life— early attachments have been broken— the death of friends I loved has fo

clouded

clouded my days; that neither the beams of profperity, nor even thofe of benevolence, can diffipate the gloom; but I am not loft in a thick fog.—My ftate of mind rather refembles the fcene before you, it is quiet—I am weaned from the world, but not difgufted—for I can ftill do good—and in futurity a fun will rife to cheer my heart.—Beyond the night of death, I hail the dawn of an eternal day! I mention my ftate of mind to you, that I may tell you what fupports me.

The feftivity within, and the placidity without, led my thoughts naturally to the fource from whence my comfort fprings—to the Great Beftower of every blefling. Prayer, my children, is the deareft privilege of man, and the fupport of a feeling heart. Mine has too often been wounded by ingratitude; my fellow-creatures, whom I have fondly loved, have neglected me—I have heard their

laft

laſt ſigh, and thrown my eyes round an empty world; but then more particularly feeling the preſence of my Creator, I poured out my ſoul before Him—and was no longer alone!—I now daily contemplate His wonderful goodneſs; and, though at an awful diſtance, try to imitate Him. This view of things is a ſpur to activity, and a conſolation in diſappointment.

There is in fact a conſtant inter-courſe kept up with the Creator, when we learn to conſider Him, as the fountain of truth, which our underſtand-ing naturally thirſts after. But His goodneſs brings Him ſtill more on a level with our bounded capacities—for we trace it in every work of mercy, and feel, in ſorrow particularly, His fatherly care. Every bleſſing is doubled when we ſuppoſe it comes from Him, and afflictions almoſt loſe their name when we believe they are ſent to correct, not cruſh us.—Whilſt we are alive

I   to

to gratitude and admiration, we muft adore God.

The human foul is fo framed, that goodnefs and truth muft fill it with ineffable pleafure, and the nearer it approaches to perfection, the more earneftly will it purfue thofe virtues, difcerning more clearly their beauty.

The Supreme Being dwells in the univerfe. He is as effentially prefent to the wicked as to the good; but the latter delight in His prefence, and try to pleafe Him, whilft the former fhrink from a Judge, who is of too pure a nature to behold iniquity.—The wicked wifh for the rocks to cover them, mountains, or the angry fea, which we the other day furveyed, to hide them from the prefence of that Being—in whofe prefence only they could find joy. You feel emotions that incite you to do good; and painful ones difturb you, when you have refifted the faithful internal monitor. The wifer, and the better

G 3   you

you grow, the more vifible, if I may ufe the expreffion, will God become— For wifdom confifts in fearching Him out—and goodnefs in endeavouring to copy his attributes.

To attain any thing great, a model muft be held up to exercife our under-ftanding, and engage our affections. A view of the difinterefted goodnefs of God is therefore calculated to touch us more than can be conceived by a depraved mind. When the love of God is fhed abroad in our hearts; true courage will animate our conduct, for nothing can hurt thofe who truft in Him. If the defire of acting right is ever prefent with us, if admiration of goodnefs fills our fouls; we may be faid to pray conftantly. And if we try to do juftice to all our fellow-creatures, and even to the brute crea-tion; and affift them as far as we can, we prove whofe fervants we are, and whofe laws we tranfcribe in our lives.

Never

Never be very anxious, when you pray, what *words* to use; regulate your *thoughts*; and recollect that virtue calms the passions, gives clearness to the understanding, and opens it to pleasures that the thoughtless and vicious have not a glimpse of. You must, believe me, be acquainted with God to find peace, to rise superior to worldly temptations. Habitual devotion is of the utmost consequence to our happiness, as what oftenest occupies the thoughts will influence our actions. But, observe what I say,—*that* devotion is mockery and selfishness, which does not improve our moral character.

Men, of old, prayed to the devil, sacrificed their children to him; and committed every kind of barbarity and impurity. But we who serve a long-suffering God should pity the weakness of our fellow-creatures; we must not beg for mercy and not shew it; —we must not acknowledge that we have offended, without trying to avoid

G 4   doing

doing fo in future. We are to deal with our fellow-creatures as we expect to be dealt with. This is practical prayer!—Thofe who practife it feel frequently fublime pleafures, and lively hopes animate them in this vale of tears; that feem a foretafte of the felicity they will enjoy, when the underftanding is more enlightened, and the affections properly regulated.

To-morrow I will take you to vifit the fchool-miftrefs of the village, and relate her ftory, to enforce what I have been faying.

Now you may go and dance one or two dances; and I will join you after I have taken a walk, which I wifh to enjoy alone.

CHAP.

C H A P. XVI.

The Benefits arising from Devotion.—
The History of the Village School-
mistress.—Fatal Effects of Inattention
to Expences, in the History of Mr.
Lofty.

THE next morning Mrs. Mason
desired the children to get their
work, and draw near the table whilst
she related the promised history; and
in the afternoon, if the weather be
fine, they were to visit the village
school-mistress.

Her father, the honourable Mr.
Lofty, was the youngest son of a
noble family; his education had been
liberal, though his fortune was small.
His relations, however, seemed determined to push him forward in life,
before he disobliged them by marrying
G 5　　　　　　the

the daughter of a country clergyman, an accomplished, sensible woman.

Some time after the birth of his daughter Anna, his elder brother, the Earl of Caermarthen, was reconciled to him; but this reconciliation only led him into expences, which his limited fortune could not bear. Mr. Lofty had a high sense of honour, and rather a profuse turn; he was, beside, a very humane man, and gave away much more than he could afford to give, when his compassion was excited. He never did a mean action; but sometimes an ostentatious pride tarnished the lustre of very splendid ones, made them appear to judicious eyes, more like tinsel, than gold. I will account for it. His first impulse arose from sensibility, and the second from an immoderate desire of human applause: for he seemed not to be alive to devotional feelings, or to have that rock to rest on, which will support a frail being, and give

4   true

true dignity to a character, though all nature combined to crush it.

Mrs. Lofty was not a shining character—but I will read you a part of a letter, which her daughter, the lady we are to visit, wrote to me.

" This being the anniversary of
" the day on which an ever loved,
" and much revered parent was re-
" leased from the bondage of morta-
" lity, I observe it with particular
" seriousness, and with gratitude; for
" her sorrows were great, her trials
" severe—but her conduct was blame-
" less: yet the world admired her
" not; her silent, modest virtues,
" were not formed to attract the
" notice of the injudicious crowd,
" and her understanding was not bril-
" liant enough to excite admiration.
" But she was regardless of the opi-
" nion of the world; she sought her
" reward in the source from whence
" her virtue was derived—and she
" found it.—He, who, for wise and

G 6   " merciful

" merciful purpoſes, ſuffered her to
" be afflicted, ſupported her under
" her trials; thereby calling forth the
" exerciſe of thoſe virtues with which
" He had adorned her gentle ſoul;
" and imparting to her a degree
" of heart-felt comfort, which no
" earthly bleſſing could afford."

This amiable parent died when
Anna was near eighteen, and left her
to the care of her father, whoſe high
ſpirit ſhe had imbibed. However, the
religious principles which her mother
had inſtilled regulated her notions of
honour, and ſo elevated her character,
that her heart was regulated by her
underſtanding.

Her father who had inſenſibly in-
volved himſelf in debt, after her mother's death, tried many different
ſchemes of life, all of which, at
firſt wore a promiſing aſpect; but
wanting that ſuppleneſs of temper,
that enables people to riſe in the
world, his ſtruggles, inſtead of ex-
tricating,

tricating, funk him ftill deeper. Wanting alfo the fupport of religion, he became four, eafily irritated, and almoft hated a world whofe applaufe he had once eagerly courted. His affairs were at laft in fuch a defperate ftate, that he was obliged, reluctantly, to accept of an invitation from his brother, who with his wife, a weak fine lady, intended to fpend fome time on the continent; his daughter was, of courfe, to be of the party.

The reftraint of obligations did not fuit his temper, and feeling himfelf dependent, he imagined every one meant to infult him.

Some farcafms were thrown out one day by a gentleman, in a large company; they were not perfonal, yet he took fire. His fore mind was eafily hurt, he refented them; and heated by wine, they both faid more than their cool reafon would have fuggefted. Mr. Lofty imagined his honour was wounded, and the next morning fent him a challenge—They met—and he
killed

killed his antagonist, who, dying, pardoned him, and declared that the sentiments which had given him so much offence, fell from him by accident, and were not levelled at any person.

The dying man lamented, that the thread of a thoughtless life had been so suddenly snapped—the name of his wife and children he could not articulate, when something like a prayer for them escaped his livid lips, and shook his exhausted frame—The blood flowed in a copious stream—vainly did Mr. Lofty endeavour to staunch it—the heart lost its vital nourishment—and the soul escaped as he pressed the hand of his destroyer.—Who, when he found him breathless, ran home, and rushed in a hurry into his own chamber. The dead man's image haunted his imagination—he started—imagined that he was at his elbow—and shook the hand that had received the dying grasp—yet still it was pressed, and the pressure entered into his very soul—On the table lay

two

two piftols, he caught up one,—and
fhot himfelf.—The report alarmed the
family.—the fervants and his daughter,
for his brother was not at home, broke
open the door,—and fhe faw the dreadful fight! As there was ftill fome
appearance of life, a trembling ray—
fhe fupported the body, and fent for
affiftance. But he foon died in her
arms without fpeaking, before the
fervant returned with a furgeon.

Horror feized her, another piftol lay
charged on the table, fhe caught it
up, but religion held her hand—fhe
knelt down by a dead father, and prayed to a fuperior one. Her mind grew
calmer—yet ftill fhe paffionately wifhed
fhe had but heard him fpeak, or that
fhe had conveyed comfort to his de-
parting fpirit—where, where would it
find comfort? again fhe was obliged
to have recourfe to prayer.

After the death of her father, her
aunt treated her as if fhe were a mere
depend-

dependent on her bounty; and expected her to be an humble companion
in every fenfe of the word. The
vifitors took the tone from her ladyfhip,
and numberlefs were the mortifications
fhe had to bear.

The entrance of a perfon about bufinefs interrupted the narration; but
Mrs. Mafon promifed to refume it
after dinner.

CHAP. XVII.

The Benefits arifing from Devotion—
The Hiftory of the Village School-
miftrefs concluded.

AS foon as the cloth was removed,
Mrs. Mafon concluded the narration; and the girls forgot their fruit
whilft they were liftening to the fequel.

Anna endured this treatment fome
years, and had an opportunity of acquiring a knowledge of the world and
her own heart. She vifited her mother's

ther's father, and would have remained with him; but she determined not to lessen the small pittance which he had anxiously saved out of a scanty income for two other grand-children. She thought continually of her situation, and found, on examining her understanding, that the fashionable circle in which she moved, could not at any rate have afforded her much satisfaction, or even amusement; though the neglect and contempt that she met with rendered her very uncomfortable. She had her father's spirit of independence, and determined to shake of the galling yoke which she had long struggled with, and try to earn her own subsistence. Her acquaintance expostulated with her, and represented the miseries of poverty, and the mortifications and difficulties that she would have to encounter. Let it be so, she replied, it is much preferable to swelling the train of the proud or vicious great, and despising myself for bearing their impertinence,

for

for eating their bitter bread;—better, indeed, is a dinner of herbs with contentment. My wants are few. When I am my own miſtreſs, the cruſt I earn will be ſweet, and the water that moiſtens it will not be mingled with tears of ſorrow or indignation.

To ſhorten my ſtory; ſhe came to me, after ſhe had attempted ſeveral plans, and requeſted my advice. She would not accept of any conſiderable favour, and declared that the greateſt would be, to put her in a way of ſupporting herſelf, without forfeiting her highly valued independence. I knew not what to adviſe; but whilſt I was debating the matter with myſelf, I happened to mention, that we were in want of a ſchool-miſtreſs. She eagerly adopted the plan, and perſevering in it theſe laſt ten years, I find her a moſt valuable acquiſition to our ſociety.

She was formed to ſhine in the moſt brilliant circle—yet ſhe relinquiſhed it, and patiently labours to improve the
children

children confiigned to her management, and tranquilize her own mind. She fucceeds in both.

She lives indeed alone, and has all day only the fociety of children; yet fhe enjoys many true pleafures; dependence on God is her fupport, and devotion her comfort. Her lively affections are therefore changed into a love of virtue and truth: and thefe exalted fpeculations have given an uncommon dignity to her manners; for fhe feems above the world, and its trifling commotions. At her meals, gratitude to Heaven fupplies the place of fociety. She has a tender, focial heart, and, as fhe cannot fweeten her folitary draught, by expreffing her good wifhes to her fellow creatures, an ejaculation to Heaven for the welfare of her friends is the fubftitute. This circumftance I heard her mention to her grandfather, who fometimes vifits her.

I will now make fome alteration in my drefs, for when I vifit thofe who
have

have been reduced from their original place in fociety by misfortunes, I always attend a little to ceremony; left too much familiarity fhould appear like difrefpect.

———

CHAP. XVIII.

Vifit to the School-miftrefs.—True and falfe Pride.

THEIR drefs was foon adjufted, and the girls plucked flowers to adorn themfelves, and a nofegay to prefent to the fchool-miftrefs, whofe garden was but fmall.

They met the children juft releafed from confinement; the fwarm came humming round Mrs. Mafon, endeavouring to catch her eye, and obtain the notice they were fo proud of. The girls made their beft courtefies, blufhing; and the boys hung down their heads,

heads, and kicked up the duſt, in ſcraping a bow of reſpect.

They found their miſtreſs preparing to drink tea, to refreſh herſelf after the toils of the day; and, with the eaſe peculiar to well-bred people, ſhe quickly enabled them to partake of it, by giving the tea-board a more ſociable appearance.

The harveſt-home was ſoon the ſubject of converſation, and the harper was mentioned. The family pride of the Welſh, ſaid Anna, has often diverted me; I have frequently heard the inhabitants of a little hut, that could ſcarcely be diſtinguiſhed from the pig-ſty, which ſtood in the front of it, boaſt of their anceſtors and deſpiſe trade. They have informed me, that one branch of their family built the middle aiſle of the church; that another beautified the chancel, and gave the ten commandments, which blaze there in letters of gold. Some rejoice that their forefathers ſleep in the moſt con-

ſpicious

fpicuous tombs—and that their afhes have an infcription to point out where they are returning to their mother earth. And thofe graves, which only a little ftone at the head gives confequence to, are adorned every Sunday with flowers, or ever-greens. We perceive, in all the various cuftoms of men, a defire to live in the paft and in the future, if I may be allowed the expreffion.

Mrs. Mafon then obferved, that of all the fpecies of pride which carry a man out of himfelf, family pride was the moft beneficial to fociety. Pride of wealth produces vanity and oftentation; but that of blood feems to infpire high notions of honour, and to banifh meannefs. Yet it is productive of many ill confequences, the moft obvious is, that it renders individuals refpectable to the generality, whofe merit is only reflected: and fometimes the want of this accidental advantage throws the moft fhining perfonal virtues

tues and abilities into obfcurity. In weak minds this pride degenerates into the moft defpicable folly; and the wife will not condefcend to accept of fame at fecond-hand, replied Anna. We ought to be proud of our original, but we fhould trace it to our Heavenly Father, who breathed into us the breath of life.——We are his children when we try to refemble Him, when we are convinced that truth and goodnefs muft conftitute the very effence of the foul; and that the purfuit of them will produce happinefs, when the vain diftinctions of mortals will fade away, and their pompous efcutcheons moulder with more vulgar duft! But remember, my young friends, virtue is immortal; and goodnefs arifes from a quick perception of truth, and actions conformable to the conviction.

Different fubjects beguiled the time, till the clofing evening admonifhed them to return home; and they departed reluctantly, filled with refpect.

CHAP.

CHAP. XIX.

Charity.—The Hiſtory of Peggy and her Family.—The Sailor's Widow.

I HAVE often remarked to you, ſaid Mrs. Maſon, one morning, to her pupils, that we are all dependent on each other; and this dependence is wiſely ordered by our Heavenly Father, to call forth many virtues, to exerciſe the beſt affections of the human heart, and fix them into habits. While we impart pleaſure we receive it, and feel the grandeur of our immortal ſoul, as it is conſtantly ſtruggling to ſpread itſelf into futurity.

Perhaps the greateſt pleaſure I have ever received, has ariſen from the habitual exerciſe of charity, in its various branches: the view of a diſtreſſed object has made me now think of converſing about one branch of it, that of giving alms.

You

You know Peggy, the young girl whom I wish to have most about my person; I mean, I wish it for her own sake, that I may have an opportunity of improving her mind, and cultivating a good capacity. As to attendance, I never give much trouble to any fellow-creature; for I choose to be independent of caprice and artificial wants; unless indeed, when I am sick; then, I thankfully receive the assistance I would willingly give to others in the same situation. I believe I have not in the world a more faithful friend than Peggy; and her earnest desire to please me gratifies my benevolence, for I always observe with delight the workings of a grateful heart.

I lost a darling child, said Mrs. Mason, smothering a sigh, in the depth of winter—death had before deprived me of her father, and when I lost my child—he died again.

The wintery prospects suiting the temper of my soul, I have sat look-

H   ing

ing at a wide wafte of tractlefs fnow for hours; and the heavy fullen fog, that the feeble rays of the fun could not pierce, gave me back an image of my mind. I was unhappy, and the fight of dead nature accorded with my feelings—for all was dead to me.

As the fnow began to melt, I took a walk, and obferved the birds hopping about with drooping wings, or mute on the leafelefs boughs. The mountain, whofe fides had loft the fnow, looked black; yet ftill fome remained on the fummit, and formed a contraft to diverfify the dreary profpect.

I walked thoughtfully along, when the appearance of a poor man, who did not beg, ftruck me very forcibly. His fhivering limbs were fcarcely fheltered from the cold by the tattered garments that covered him; and he had a fharp, famifhed look. I ftretched out my hand with fome relief in it, I would not enquire into
the

the particulars of such obvious distress. The poor wretch caught my hand, and hastily dropping on his knees, thanked me in an extacy, as if he had almost lost sight of hope, and was overcome by the sudden relief. His attitude, for I cannot bear to see a fellow-creature kneel, and eager thanks, oppressed my weak spirits, so that I could not for a moment ask him any more questions; but as soon as I recollected myself, I learned from him the misfortunes that had reduced him to such extreme distress, and he hinted, that I could not easily guess the good I had done. I imagined from this hint that he was meditating his own destruction when I saw him, to spare himself the misery of seeing his infant perish,—starved to death, in every sense of the word.

I will now hasten to the sequel of the account. His wife had lately had a child, she was very ill at the time,

and

and want of proper food, and a de-
fence againſt the inclemency of the
weather, hurried her out of the world.
The poor child, Peggy, had ſucked
in diſeaſe and nouriſhment together,
and now even that wretched ſource
had failed—the breaſt was cold that
had afforded the ſcanty ſupport;
and the little innocent ſmiled, un-
conſcious of its miſery. I ſent for
her, added Mrs. Maſon, and her
father dying a few years after, ſhe has
ever been a favourite charge of mine,
and nurſing of her, in ſome meaſure,
diſpelled the gloom in which I had
been almoſt loſt.—Ah! my children,
you know not how many, " houſe-
leſs heads bide the pitileſs ſtorm!"

I received ſoon after a leſſon of
reſignation from a poor woman, who
was a practical philoſopher.

She had loſt her huſband, a ſailor,
and loſt his wages alſo, as ſhe could
not prove his death. She came to
me to beg ſome pieces of ſilk, to
make

make some pin-cushions for the boarders of a neighbouring school. Her lower weeds were patched with different coloured rags; but they spoke not variety of wretchedness, on the contrary, they shewed a mind so content, that want, and bodily pain, did not prevent her thinking of the opinion of casual observers. This woman lost a husband and a child suddenly, and her daily bread was precarious.—I cheered the widow's heart, and my own was not quite solitary.

But I am growing melancholy, whilst I am only desirous of pointing out to you how very beneficial charity is—because it enables us to find comfort when all our worldly comforts are blighted: besides, when our bowels yearn to our fellow-creatures, we feel that the love of God dwelleth in us—and then we cannot always go on our way sorrowing.

H 3   CHAP.

CHAP. XX.

Visit to Mrs. Trueman—The Use of Accomplishments—Virtue the Soul of all.

IN the afternoon they visited Mrs. Trueman unexpectedly, and found her sitting in the garden playing to her children, who danced on the green sod. She approached to receive them, and laid aside her guitar; but, after some conversation, Mrs. Mason desired her to take it up again, and the girls joined in the request. While she was singing Mary whispered Mrs. Mason, that she would give the world to be able to sing as well. The whisper was not so low but a part of it reached Mrs. Truman's ears, who said to her, smiling, my young friend, you value accomplishments much too highly—they may give grace to virtue— but are nothing without
solid

folid worth.—Indeed, I may fay more, for any thing like perfection in the arts cannot be attained, where a relifh; nay, a delight in what is true and noble is wanting. A fuperficial obferver may be pleafed with a picture in which fine colours predominate; and quick movements in mufic may tickle the ear, though they never reach the heart: but it is the fimple ftrain which affection animates, that we liften to with intereft and delight. Mr. Trueman has a tafte for the fine arts; and I wifh in every thing to be his companion. His converfation has improved my judgment, and the affection an intimate knowledge of his virtues has infpired, increafes the love which I feel for the whole human race. He lives retired from the world; to amufe him after the bufinefs of the day is over, and my babes afleep, I fing to him. A defire to pleafe, and the pleafure I read in his eyes, give to my mufic energy and

tendernefs.

tenderneſs. When he is ruffled
by worldly cares, I try to ſmooth
his wrinkled brow, and think mine
a voice of melody, when it has had
that effect.

Very true, replied Mrs. Maſon,
accompliſhments ſhould be cultivated
to render us pleaſing to our domeſtic
friends; virtue is neceſſary; it muſt
ever be the foundation of our peace
and uſefulneſs; but when we are capable of affection, we wiſh to have
ſomething peculiar to ourſelves. We
ſtudy the taſte of our friends, and
endeavour to conform to it; but, in
doing ſo, we ought rather to improve
our own abilities than ſervilely to copy
theirs. Obſerve, my dear girls, Mrs.
Trueman's diſtinction, her accompliſhments are for her friends, her
virtues for the world in general.

I ſhould think myſelf vain, and my
ſoul little, anſwered Mrs. Trueman,
if the applauſe of the whole world, on
the ſcore of abilities, which did not
add

add any real luftre to my character,
could afford me matter of exultation.
The approbation of my own heart,
the humble hope of pleafing the Moft
High, elevates my foul; and I feel,
that in a future ftate, I may enjoy an
unfpeakable degree of happinefs, though
I now only experience a faint foretafte.
Next to thefe fublime emotions, which
I cannot defcribe, and the joy refulting
from doing good; I am happy when
I can amufe thofe I love; it is not
then vanity, but tendernefs, that fpurs
me on, and my fongs, my drawings,
my every action, has fomething of
my heart in it. When I can add to
the innocent enjoyments of my children, and improve them at the fame
time, are not my accomplifhments of
ufe? In the fame ftyle, when I vary
the pleafures of my fire-fide, I make
my hufband forget that it is a lonely
one; and he returns to look for elegance at home, elegance that he himfelf gave the polifh to; and which is

only

only affected, when it does not flow from virtuous affections.

I beg your pardon, I expatiate too long on my favorite topic; my defire to rectify your notions muft plead my excufe.

Mr. Trueman now joined them, and brought with him fome of his fineft fruit. After tea Mrs. Trueman fhewed them fome of her drawings; and, to comply with their repeated requeft, played on the harpfichord, and Mr. Trueman took his violin to accompany her. Then the children were indulged with a dance, each had her favourite tune played in turn.

As they returned home, the girls were eagerly lavifhing praifes on Mrs. Trueman; and Mary faid, I cannot tell why, but I feel fo glad when fhe takes notice of me. I never faw any one look fo good-natured, cried Caroline. Mrs. Mafon joined in the converfation. You juftly remarked that fhe is good-natured; you remem_

ber

ber her hiſtory, ſhe loves truth, and
ſhe is ever exerciſing benevolence and
love—from the inſect, that ſhe avoids
treading on, her affection may be
traced to that Being who lives for
ever.—And it is from her goodneſs her
agreeable qualities ſpring.

CHAP. XXI.

*The Benefit of bodily Pain.—Fortitude
the Baſis of Virtue.—The Folly of
Irreſolution.*

THE children had been playing
in the garden for ſome time,
whilſt Mrs. Maſon was reading alone.
But ſhe was ſuddenly alarmed by the
cries of Caroline, who ran into the
room in great diſtreſs. Mary quickly
followed, and explaining the matter
ſaid, that her ſiſter had accidently
H 6   diſturbed

disturbed some wasps, who were terrified, and of course stung her. Remedies were applied to assuage the pain; yet all the time she uttered the loudest and most silly complaints, regardless of the uneasiness she gave those who were exerting themselves to relieve her.

In a short time the smart abated, and then her friend thus addressed her, with more than usual gravity. I am sorry to see a girl of your age weep on account of bodily pain; it is a proof of a weak mind—a proof that you cannot employ your-self about things of consequence. How often must I tell you that the Most High is educating us for eternity?

" The term virtue, comes from a
" word signifying strength. Fortitude
" of mind is, therefore, the basis of
" every virtue, and virtue belongs to
" a being, that is weak in its nature,
" and strong only in will and reso-
" lution."

Children

Children early feel bodily pain, to
habituate them to bear the conflicts
of the foul, when they become reafonable creatures. This, I fay, is
the firft trial, and I like to fee that
proper pride which ftrives to conceal
its fufferings. Thofe who, when
young, weep if the leaft trifle an-
noys them, will never, I fear, have
fufficient ftrength of mind, to encounter all the miferies that can afflict
the body, rather than act meanly to
avoid them. Indeed, this feems to
be the effential difference between a
great and a little mind: the former
knows how to endure—whilft the
latter fuffers an immortal foul to be
depreffed, loft in its abode; fuffers
the inconveniencies which attack the
one to overwhelm the other. The
foul would always fupport the body, if
its fuperiority was felt, and invigorated
by exercife. The Almighty, who
never afflicts but to produce fome
good end, firft fends difeafes to children

dren to teach them patience and fortitude; and when by degrees they
have learned to bear them, they have
acquired some virtue.

In the same manner, cold or
hunger, when accidentally encoun-
tered, are not evils; they make *us
feel what wretches feel*, and teach us
to be tender-hearted. Many of your
fellow-creatures daily bear what you
cannot for a moment endure without
complaint. Besides, another advantage arises from it, after you have
felt hunger, you will not be very
anxious to choose the particular kind
of food that is to satisfy it. You
will then be freed from a frivolous
care.

When it is necessary to take a nau-
seous draught, swallow it at once,
and do not make others sick whilst
you are hesitating, though you know
that you ought to take it. If a tooth
is to be drawn, or any other disagreeable operation to be performed,
determine

determine refolutely that it fhall be done immediately; and debate not, when you clearly fee the ftep that you ought to take. If I fee a child act in this way, I am ready to embrace it, my foul yearns for it—I perceive the dawning of a character that will be ufeful to fociety, as it prepares its foul for a nobler field of action.

Believe me, it is the patient endurance of pain, that will enable you to refift your paffions; after you have borne bodily pain, you will have firmnefs enough to fuftain the ftill more excruciating agonies of the mind. You will not, to banifh momentary cares, plunge into diffipation, nor to efcape a prefent inconvenience, forget that you fhould hold faft virtue as the only fubftantial good.

I fhould not value the affection of a perfon who would not bear pain and hunger to ferve me; nor is that benevolence warm, which fhrinks

from

from encountering difficulties, when it is neceſſary, in order to be uſeful to any fellow creature.

There is a juſt pride, a noble ambition in ſome minds, that I greatly admire. I have ſeen a little of it in Mary! for whilſt ſhe pities others, ſhe imagines that ſhe could bear their inconveniences herſelf; and ſhe ſeems to feel more uneaſineſs, when ſhe obſerves the ſufferings of others, than I could ever trace on her countenance under the immediate preſſure of pain.

Remember you are to bear patiently the infirmities of the weakeſt of your fellow-creatures; but to yourſelves you are not to be equally indulgent,

CHAP.

CHAP. XXII.

Journey to London.

THE girls were vifibly improved; an air of intelligence began to animate Caroline's fine features; and benevolence gave her eyes the humid fparkle which is fo beautiful and engaging. The intereft that we take in the fate of others, attaches them to ourfelves;—thus Caroline's goodnefs infpired more affection than her beauty.

Mary's judgment grew every day clearer; or, more properly fpeaking, fhe acquired experience; and her lively feelings fixed the conclufions of reafon in her mind. Whilft Mrs. Mafon was rejoicing in their apparent improvement, fhe received a letter from their father, requefting her to allow his daughters to fpend the winter in town, as he wifhed to procure them the beft mafters, an advantage that the country did not afford. With reluctance

fhe

she confented, determining to remain with them a short time; and preparations were quickly made for the journey.

The wished for morning arrived, and they set off in a tumult of spirits; sorry to leave the country, yet delighted with the prospect of visiting the metropolis. This hope soon dried the tears which had bedewed their cheeks; for the parting with Mrs. Mason was not anticipated. The autumnal views were new to them; they saw the hedges exhibit various colours, and the trees stripped of their leaves; but they were not disposed to moralize.

For some time after their arrival, every thing they saw excited wonder and admiration; and not till they were a little familiarized with the new objects, did they ask reasonable questions.

Several presents recruited their purses; and they requested Mrs. Mason.

fon to allow them to buy fome trifles
they were in want of. The requeft
was modeft, and fhe complied.

C H A P. XXIII.

*Charity.—Shopping.— The diftreffed Sta-
tioner.—Mifchievous Confequences of
delaying Payment.*

AS they walked in fearch of a
fhop, they both determined to
purchafe pocket-books; but their friend
defired them not to fpend all their
money at once, as they would meet
many objects of charity in the nume-
rous ftreets of the metropolis. I do not
wifh you, fhe continued, to relieve every
beggar that you cafually meet; yet
fhould any one attract your attention,
obey the impulfe of your heart, which
will lead you to pay them for exercifing
your

your compaffion, and do not fuffer the whifpers of felfifhnefs, that they may be impofters, to deter you. However, I would have you give but a trifle when you are not certain the diftrefs is real, and reckon it given for pleafure. I for my part would rather be deceived five hundred times, than doubt once without reafon.

They ftopped at a fmall fhop, Mrs. Mafon always fought out fuch; for, faid fhe, I may help thofe who perhaps want affiftance; bargains I never feek, for I wifh every one to receive the juft value for their goods.

In the fhop which they chanced to enter, they did not find the kind of pocket-book that they had previoufly fixed on, and therefore wifhed precipitately to leave it; but were detained by their more confiderate friend. While they had been turning over the trinkets, the countenance of the woman, who ferved them, caught her eye, and fhe obferved her eager manner of recom-
mending

mending the books. You have given
much unneceffary trouble, faid fhe,
to the miftrefs of the fhop; the books
are better, and more expenfive than
you intended to purchafe, but I will
make up the deficiency. A beam of
pleafure enlivened the woman's fwollen
eyes; and Mrs. Mafon, in the mild
accents of compaffion, faid, if it is
not an impertinent queftion, will you
tell me from what caufe your vifible
diftrefs arifes? perhaps I may have
it in my power to relieve you —The
woman burft into tears.--Indeed, Madam, you have already relieved me;
for the money you have laid out will
enable me to procure fome food for
my poor little grandchildren, and to
fend a meal to their poor father, who is
now confined for debt, though a more
honeft man never breathed. Ah!
Madam, I little thought I fhould
come to this—Yefterday his wife died,
poor foul! I really believe things
going fo crofs broke her heart. He

has

has been in jail thefe five months; I could not manage the fhop, or buy what was proper to keep up the credit of it, fo bufinefs has been continually falling off; yet, if his debts were paid, he would now be here, and we fhould have money in our pockets. And what renders it more provoking, the people who owe us moft are very rich. It is true, they live in fuch a very high ftyle, and keep fuch a number of horfes and fervants, that they are often in want of money, and when they have it, they moftly have fome freak in their heads, and do not think of paying poor trades-people. At firft we were afraid to afk for payment left we fhould lofe their cuftom, and fo it proved; when we did venture, forced by neceffity, they fent to other fhops, without difcharging our de-mand.

And, my dear Madam, this is not all my grief; my fon, before his mif-fortunes, was one of the moft fober,

2   induftrious

industrious young men in London; but now he is not like the fame man. He had nothing to do in the jail, and to drive away care he learned to drink; he faid it was a comfort to forget himfelf, and he would add an oath—I never heard him fwear till then. I took pains when he was a child to teach him his prayers, and he rewarded me by being a dutiful fon. The cafe is quite altered now—he feems to have loft all natural affection —he heeds not his mother's tears. —Her fobs almoft fuffocated her, as fhe ftrove to go on—He will bring my grey hairs with forrow to the grave—and yet I pity my poor boy, he is fhut up with fuch a number of profligate wretches, who laugh at what is right. Every farthing I fend him he fpends in liquor, and ufed to make his poor wife pawn her clothes to buy him drink—fhe was happy to die, it was well for her not to live

to

to hear the babe she gave suck to
despise her!

A passion of tears relieved the sufferer, and she called her grandchildren; these innocent babes, said she, I
shall not be able to keep them, they
must go to the workhouse. If the quality did but know what they make us
poor industrious people suffer—surely
they would be more considerate.

Mrs. Mason gave her something to
supply her present wants, and promised to call on her again before she
left town.

They walked silently down two or
three streets; I hope you have learned
to think, my dear girls, said Mrs.
Mason, and that your hearts have
felt the emotions of compassion; need
I make any comments on the situation
of the poor woman we have just left.
You perceive that those who neglect
to pay their debts, do more harm
than they imagine; perhaps, indeed,
some of these very people do, what

is

is called, a noble action, give away a large sum, and are termed generous; nay, very probably, weep at a tragedy, or when reading an affecting tale. They then boast of their sensibility—when, alas! neglecting the foundation of all virtue, *justice*, they have occasioned exquisite distress;—led a poor wretch into vice; heaped misery on helpless infancy, and drawn tears from the aged widow.

CHAP. XXIV.

Visit to a poor Family in London.—Idleness the Parent of Vice.—Prodigality and Generosity incompatible.—The Pleasures of Benevolence.—True and false Motives for saving.

AFTER the impression which the story, and the sight of the family had made, was a little worn off;

I

off; Caroline begged leave to buy one
toy, and then another, till her money
was quite gone. When Mrs. Mason
found it was all expended, she looked
round for an object in distress; a poor
woman soon presented herself, and her
meagre countenance gave weight to
her tale.—A babe, as meagre, hung
at her breast, which did not seem to
contain sufficient moisture to wet its
parched lips.

On enquiry they found that she
lodged in a neighbouring garret.
Her husband had been out of employment a long time, and was now
sick. The master who had formerly
given him work, lost gradually
great part of his business; for his best
customers were grown so fond of
foreign articles, that his goods grew
old in the warehouse. Consequently
a number of hands were dismissed,
who not immediately finding employment elsewhere, were reduced
to the most extreme distress. The
truth

2

truth of this account a reputable shopkeeper attested; and he added that many of the unhappy creatures, who die unpitied at the gallows, were first led into vice by accident/ idleness.

They ascended the dark stairs, scarcely able to bear the bad smells that flew from every part of a small house, that contained in each room a family, occupied in such an anxious manner to obtain the necessaries of life, that its comforts never engaged their thoughts. The precarious meal was snatched, and the stomach did not turn, though the cloth, on which it was laid, was died in dirt. When to-morrow's bread is uncertain, who thinks of cleanliness? Thus does despair encrease the misery, and consequent disease aggravate the horrors of poverty!

They followed the woman into a low garret, that was never visited by the chearful rays of the sun.—A man,

with

with a fallow complexion, and long
beard, fat fhivering over a few cin-
ders in the bottom of a broken grate,
and two more children were on the
ground, half naked, near him, breath-
ing the fame noxious air. The gaiety
natural to their age, did not animate
their eyes, half funk in their fockets;
and, inftead of fmiles, premature
wrinkles had found a place in their
lengthened vifages. Life was nipped
in the bud; fhut up juft as it began
to unfold itfelf. " A froft, a killing
froft," had deftroyed the parent's hopes:
they feemed to come into the world
only to crawl half formed,—to fuffer,
and to die.

Mrs. Mafon defired the girls to
relieve the family; Caroline hung
down her head abafhed—wifhing the
paltry ornaments which fhe had thought-
lefsly bought, in the bottom of the fea.
Mary, meanwhile, proud of the new
privilege, emptied her purfe; and Caroline, in a fupplicating tone, entreated
Mrs. Mafon

Œconomy & Self-denial are necessary, in
every station, to enable us to be generous.

Published by J. Johnson, Sept.ʳ 1, 1791.

Mrs. Mason to allow her to give her neck-handkerchief to the little infant.

Mrs. Mason desired the woman to call on her the next day; and they left the family cheered by their bounty.

Caroline expected the reproof that soon proceeded from the mouth of her true friend. I am glad that this accident has occured, to prove to you that prodigality and generosity are incompatible. Æconomy and self-denial are necessary in every station; to enable us to be generous, and to act conformably to the rules of justice.

Mary may this night enjoy peaceful slumbers; idle fancies, foolishly indulged, will not float in her brain; she may, before she closes her eyes, thank God, for allowing her to be His instrument of mercy. Will the trifles that you have purchased, afford you such heartfelt delight, Caroline?

Selfish people save to gratify their own caprices and appetites; the be-

nevolent

nevolent curb both, to give scope to
the nobler feelings of the human heart.
When we squander money idly, we
defraud the poor, and deprive our
own souls of their most exalted food.
If you wish to be useful, govern your
desires, and wait not till distress ob-
trudes itself—search it out. In the
country it is not always attended with
such shocking circumstances as at present; but in large cities, many garrets
contain families, similar to those we
have seen this afternoon. The money spent in indulging the vain wishes
of idleness, and a childish fondness
for pretty things not regulated by
reason, would relieve the misery that
my soul shrinks back from contem-
plating.

CHAP.

CHAP. XXV.

Mrs. Mason's farewell Advice to her young Friends.

THE day before Mrs Mason was to leave her pupils, she took a hand of each, and pressing them tenderly in her own, tears started into her eyes—I tremble for you, my dear girls, for you must now practise by yourselves some of the virtues which I have been endeavouring to inculcate: and I shall anxiously wait for the summer, to see what progress you have made by yourselves.

We have conversed on several very important subjects; pray do not forget the conclusions I have drawn.

I now, as my last present, give you a book, in which I have written the subjects that we have discussed. Re-

cur

cur frequently to it, for the stories illustrating the instruction it contains, you will not feel in such a great degree the want of my personal advice. Some of the reasoning you may not thoroughly comprehend, but, as your understandings ripen, you will feel its full force.

Avoid anger; exercise compassion; and love truth. Recollect, that from religion your chief comfort must spring, and never neglect the duty of prayer. Learn from experience the comfort that arises from making known your wants and sorrows to the wisest and best of Beings, in whose hands are the issues, not only of this life, but of that which is to come.

Your father will allow you a certain stipend; you have already *felt* the pleasure of doing good; ever recollect that the wild pursuits of fancy must be conquered, to enable you to gratify benevolent wishes, and that you must practise œconomy in trifles to have

it

it in your power to be generous on great occafions. And the good you intend to do, do quickly;—for know that a trifling duty neglected, is a great fault, and the prefent time only is at your command.

You are now candidates for my friendſhip, and on your advancement in virtue my regard will in future depend. Write often to me, I will punctually anfwer your letters; but let me have the genuine fentiments of your hearts. In expreſſions of affection and refpect, do not deviate from truth to gain what you wiſh for, or to turn a period prettily.

Adieu! when you think of your friend, obferve her precepts; and let the recollection of my affection, give additional weight to the truths which I have endeavoured to, inftill; and, to re- ward my care, let me hear that you love and practice virtue.

F I N I S.

A CATALOGUE *of* BOOKS *compofed for Children and young Perfons, and generally ufed in the principal Schools and Academies in England.*

Printed for J. JOHNSON, No. 72, *St. Paul's Church-yard.*

1. An INTRODUCTION to the KNOWLEDGE of NATURE and Reading the Holy Scriptures, by Mrs. Trimmer. Price 2s. bound.

2. FABULOUS HISTORIES, teaching the proper Treatment of Animals, by the fame. Price 2s. bound.

3. L'AMI DES ENFANS, par M. Berquin, complete in 4 Volumes, with Frontifpieces. Price 12s. bound.

4. The CHILDREN's FRIEND, being a Tranflation of the above, complete in 4 Volumes, with Frontifpieces. Price 10s. bound.

5. SELECT STORIES for the Inftruction and Improvement of Children, felected from the above. Price 3s. bound.

6. The CATECHISM of NATURE, by Dr. Martinet, Profeffor of Philofophy at Zutphen. Tranflated from the Dutch, by the Rev. John Hall. Price 1s.

7. The CALENDAR of NATURE, by Dr. Aikin. Price 1s.

8. ELEMENTS of MORALITY. Tranflated from the German of the Rev. C. G. Salzmann, embellifhed with fifty Plates. 3 Vols. Price 10s. 6d. bound.

9. The NATURAL HISTORY of BIRDS; containing a Variety of Facts felected from feveral Writers, and intended for the Amufement and Inftruction of Children, 3 Volumes. Illuftrated with upwards of one hundred Copper-plates, both coloured and plain.

10. PHILOSOPHICAL AMUSEMENTS; or Eafy and Inftructive Recreations for young People. Pr. 1s.

11. YOUNG GRANDISON. A Series of Letters from young People to their Friends. Tranflated from the Dutch of Mad. Cambon, 2 Vols. 12mo. Price 6s. bound.

12. The ART of DRAWING and PAINTING in WATER COLOURS, with Cuts. Fifth Edition. Price 1s.

13. The ART of DRAWING in PERSPECTIVE, for the Use of such as are Strangers to Mathematics. To which is added, the Art of Painting upon Glass, and Drawing in Crayons; also the Art of Etching and Japanning, with Cuts. The Fourth Edition. Price 1s.

14. The ART of WRITING: containing Directions for Writing, and Copperplate Copies of all the Hands now in Use; very useful to those who have not the Instruction of a Master. By A. Serle. Price 1s.

15. GEOGRAPHY for CHILDREN: or, a short and easy Method of teaching and learning Geography; whereby Children may, in a short Time, be taught the Use of the Terrestrial Globe, and Geographical Maps; and gain a Knowledge of all the considerable Countries in the World, their Situation, Boundaries, Extent, Divisions, Rivers, chief Cities, Government, and Religion. Translated from the French of Abbot Langlet du Fresnoy. 15th Edition, greatly improved, and corrected to the Treaty of Peace in 1783. With a Table of the Latitude and Longitude of principal Places. Price 1s. 6d.

16. ÆSOP's FABLES, with instructive Morals and Reflections, adapted to all Capacities, by W. Richardson, Author of Clarissa, Grandison, &c. Illustrated with Copperplates. Price 2s. 6. bound.

17. A FATHER's INSTRUCTIONS: consisting of Moral Tales, Fables, and Reflections, designed to promote a Love of Truth, a Taste for Knowledge, and an early Acquaintance with the Works of Nature. By Thomas Percival, M. D. Price 4s.

18. MORAL and LITERARY DISSERTATIONS, on, 1. Truth and Faithfulness. 2. On Habit and Association. 3. On Inconsistency of Expectation in literary Pursuits. 4. On a Taste for the general Beauties of Nature. 5. On a Taste for the fine Arts, &c. chiefly intended as the Sequel to a Father's Instructions. By the same. Price 5s.

19. The SPEAKER; or Miscellaneous Pieces, selected from the best English Writers, and disposed under proper Heads, with a View to facilitate the

Improvement of Youth in Reading and Speaking, as well as to lead young Persons into some Acquaintance with the most valuable Writers, and impress upon their Minds Sentiments of Honour and Virtue. To which is prefixed, an Essay on Elocution. By W. Enfield, LL. D. Lecturer on the Belles Lettres, in the Academy at Warrington. Price 3s. 6d.

20. EXERCISES in ELOCUTION; selected from the best Authors, being a Sequel to the Speaker. By the same. Price 3s. 6d.

21. The FEMALE READER: or Miscellaneous Pieces in Prose and Verse; selected from the best Writers, and disposed under proper Heads, upon the same Plan as the SPEAKER. For the Instruction of Young Women. By M. CRESSWICK. To which is prefixed, a Preface, containing some Hints on Female Education. Price 3s. 6d. bound.

22. ENGLAND DELINEATED: or a Geographical Description of every county in England and Wales; with a concise Account of its most important Products, natural and artificial. For the Use of young Persons. By J. AIKIN, M. D. Price 5s. bound. Second Edition, corrected.

Outline Maps of the Counties of England, engraved as a Companion to the above Work, may be had bound up with it, price 7s. or separately, price 2s.

23. The STUDENT's POCKET DICTIONARY: or Compendium of Universal History, Chronology, and Biography, from the earliest Accounts to the present Time, with Authorities. In Two Parts. Part I. containing a Compendium of universal History; Part II. a Compendium of universal Biography. By THO. MORTIMER, Esq. The Second Edition, with considerable Emendations and Additions. Pr. 4s. bound.

24. SACRED HISTORY, selected from the Scriptures; with Annotations and Reflections, designed for Young People, particularly calculated to facilitate the Study of the Scriptures in Schools and Families, By Mrs. Trimmer. 6 Vols. Price 18s. in Boards, 21s. bound in Sheep roll'd, or 24s. in Calf and lettered.